A Hy & Drye Mystery

MAISIE FRANKLIN

Printed in the United States.
Wagging Tales Press
First Printing, 2026
ISBN: 978-1-962191-14-2

CHAPTER ONE

I'd survived stakeouts, shootouts, and three ex-wives, but nothing prepared me for the pure hell of my daughter trying to sign me up for goat yoga.

Retirement, my ass.

I scratched my jaw, feeling the wiry bristles of my mustache — grizzled enough to have its own backstory, just like the rest of me. At sixty-eight, I wasn't ready for shuffleboard and all-you-can-eat pudding cups, but try telling that to my daughter, Gloria.

Instead of embracing my golden years with tai chi and decaf, I'd taken up a hobby that suited me just fine: sitting at the Palm Vista Golf Club's bar, drinking coffee like it was a police interrogation, and quietly observing the high crimes and misdemeanors of the rich and restless.

I leaned against the polished mahogany, my stocky frame settling in like a well-worn jacket. The air reeked of freshly mowed greens, expensive cologne, and regret — mostly from the poor schmucks who'd bet against their own golf game. Golf clubs were just country clubs with an athletic alibi, and I didn't trust a single person in plaid pants.

Speaking of which —

"Sure, sure, Marjorie," Roger Whitaker chuckled. His belly strained against a polo shirt that had lost a battle with his midsection. His plaid pants were so loud they should've come with a noise complaint. "Last night was certainly a hole-in-one, if you catch my drift."

Marjorie, a woman with the look of a Botoxed tabby cat, shot him a scandalized glare. "Roger, keep your voice down! What if someone hears?"

"Who'd believe it?" Roger winked. "Just two old friends discussing... golf techniques."

Marjorie snorted, rolling her eyes.

I barely had to squint through my detective instincts to see the flashing neon sign over their heads:

GUILTY OF SOMETHING.

Now, I'd been retired for a few years, but I still had the nose for a good mystery — and the only thing that stood out worse than a bad lie was two people who thought they were good at it.

I adjusted my stance, pretending to study a brochure on putter grips while my ears honed in like a radio scanning for police chatter.

My elbow rested on the bar, next to a folded copy of the Miami Herald, left behind by some other patron.

Half paying attention, I let my eyes drift across the front-page headline:

SEC LAUNCHES INVESTIGATION INTO CEO OF CENTURION ENTERPRISES

Below it was a grainy photograph of some bigwig in a suit, mid-stride, turning his head away from the camera like he wanted no part of it. He wasn't fast enough. I could still make out the sharp set of his jaw, a receding hairline, and — most notably — a gaudy ring glinting on his right hand.

"Marjorie, darling," Roger crooned, oblivious to my eavesdropping. "I must admit, our little sessions have improved my... stamina on the course."

"Stamina, indeed," Marjorie murmured, her lashes fluttering enough to create a light breeze.

I made a noise in the back of my throat. The only thing more predictable than death and taxes? Old men who thought they were George Clooney but were more like Danny DeVito in a leisure suit.

"Scandalous," I muttered to myself, savoring the word like a fine bourbon. I could already see tomorrow's headline: 'Local Golf Pro Caught Playing More Than Just the Back Nine!'

Marjorie leaned in, her eyes darting around, then settling on me. "Shh! You never know who's listening."

Roger laughed. "Relax. The only thing Hy Reynolds is catching these days are Zs on the clubhouse sofa."

I sipped my coffee and smirked. They had no idea that retirement had only made me better at my job.

The thing about police work is that after decades of reading liars, trailing suspects, and connecting dots nobody else saw, the habit doesn't go away. It's like muscle memory.

Roger and Marjorie had my attention now, and my imagination teed off — launching me straight into a bunker of possibilities.

A secret affair? Hidden debts? A scandal bubbling beneath the surface like a geyser ready to blow?

"Imagine," I mused, "a clandestine love affair, right here in the sand traps of suburbia."

Of course, knowing my luck, they were probably just two golf nerds swapping pointers on their short game.

Still, old habits died hard.

And I liked a good mystery.

A voice behind me scolded. "Really, Dad?"

I froze. My instincts, sharpened from years of catching criminals in their lies, recognized that tone immediately: Long-suffering. Patient. Mildly homicidal.

Gloria.

I turned, greeted by the sight of my daughter standing with her hands on her hips. Not the tailored power stance of a CEO, but the battle-ready posture of a woman who had wrangled kids, groceries, and her father's nonsense — all in one afternoon.

Her windblown hair was shoved into a haphazard ponytail, and the outline of a juice box stain decorated her sleeve — clear evidence of a day spent in the trenches of suburban warfare.

She eyed me like I was a kid caught sneaking cookies before dinner.

"Good grief," she sighed, shaking her head. "You're like a truffle pig rooting for scandal."

I leaned against the bar, unimpressed. "I'm just observing human nature."

"Observing?" She crossed her arms. "Or stirring the pot until it boils over and scalds everyone within a ten-foot radius?"

I shrugged. "To-MAY-to, to-MAH-to."

She exhaled through her nose, the way she used to when I'd caught her sneaking out past curfew as a teenager. "Dad, do you realize you're about as inconspicuous as a flamingo at a penguin party?"

"That's offensive," I said, wounded. "I blend."

She pinched the bridge of her nose. "The last time you 'blended,' we ended up being banned from the neighborhood watch meeting because you convinced Mrs. Henderson her cat was an undercover spy."

"I'm telling you, that Russian Blue had unusually shifty eyes."

Gloria leveled me with The Look. The one that had the uncanny power to make me regret every decision leading up to that moment.

"Look, Dad," she softened her voice, her eyes scanning mine. "Retirement hasn't been easy on you. Especially without Mom. I get it. But there are better ways to occupy your time than playing Sherlock Holmes at the golf club."

"You're saying that like it's an option."

"It is an option," she said, stepping closer. "Or… you can keep this up, and I'll have no choice but to follow through on my promise."

I frowned. "What promise?"

Gloria folded her arms. "Shady Pines."

Shady Pines.

The assisted living facility.

A fate worse than death.

"Gloria," I said carefully, "you wound me."

She arched a brow. "You brought this on yourself."

I sighed dramatically, tossing a glance to the heavens. "Fine. No more sleuthing. No more eavesdropping. No more mild espionage. Happy?"

She considered this. "I'll take 'mild' espionage over 'full-blown neighborhood spy.'"

"Deal."

Her shoulders loosened, and she smiled. "Thank you."

"Anything for my girl."

We stood there for a moment, the late afternoon sun casting long shadows over the green. I could still smell the freshly cut grass, hear the distant *thwack* of a golf club meeting its target.

I should've been satisfied.

But I wasn't.

Because old detectives don't just stop detecting.

And something told me trouble was brewing, whether I went looking for it or not.

Who knew it would stand all of five-foot-nothing and come wrapped in a cardigan?

***

A good librarian knows that the most important things in life are cataloged, cross-referenced, and preferably wrapped in something practical — like a well-loved sweater or an airtight alibi.

That was what I told myself as I navigated the grocery store, my soft-soled shoes making no noise against the worn tile, my trusty cardigan tucked firmly around my shoulders like armor. I was, as always, on a mission. This time for prunes.

The produce section smelled faintly of citrus and Axe body spray. I lingered in front of the dried fruit display, adjusting my glasses as I scrutinized the options. Whole prunes or prune juice? It was a question as old as time — or at least as old as dietary fiber awareness.

I picked up a package and examined it with the same meticulous attention I'd once given to first-edition manuscripts at the library. The *petit d'Agen* plum, the foundation of all fine prunes, had been cultivated since the 12th century. Most people didn't appreciate the complexities of prune production, but I did.

"Excuse me, young man," I beckoned to a nearby stock boy, whose nametag declared him to be Tyler, and the source of the pungent body spray. "Have you heard any feedback on the efficacy of these prunes?"

Tyler blinked, shifting the crate of bananas in his arms like I'd asked him who signed the Magna Carta. King John of England, for inquiring minds.

"Uh… I… don't know, ma'am."

A pity. Young people these days lacked curiosity.

"Well," I pressed on, undeterred, "prunes are not just dried plums, you see. They come from a specific varietal, one that thrives in California — descended from the esteemed *petit d'Agen*, which was introduced to the region during the Gold Rush."

Tyler's eyes darted toward an exit, but I was just getting to the interesting part.

"It's fascinating, really. Did you know that commercial prune orchards are often threatened by wildfire season? The smoke affects their sugar content. This is particularly interesting when considering their laxative properties—"

But alas, I had lost him. Tyler had slipped away, abandoning me to my research like a fair-weather scholar in a difficult course.

"Kids these days," I muttered, sighing as I turned back to the prune selection.

I was about to settle my internal debate—juice or whole—when movement near the melon display caught my attention.

Mildred Jansen.

I narrowed my eyes. My neighbor. Widow. Volunteer bridge instructor. Serial late returner of borrowed books. And unless my vision was failing me, she was not alone.

I pulled my cardigan tighter and maneuvered myself behind an imposing pyramid of cantaloupes and honeydew. A sturdy, fruit-based fortress.

Mildred was laughing. Not her polite, committee-appropriate laugh. A real, hands-on-the-arm laugh. The kind that suggested secrets.

I should have brought my binoculars.

I leaned ever so slightly for a better look—just a whisper of movement. Unfortunately, my elbow *whispered* right into the precarious edge of the cantaloupe display.

The first melon teetered. Then the second. And before I could blink...

Melon mayhem.

Cantaloupes tumbled from their perch like boulders in an Indiana Jones movie—lordy, but that Harrison Ford was still a looker—rolling with slow but inevitable destruction. One clipped a stack of sweet potatoes, which promptly joined the rebellion, scattering in every direction.

I gasped, stumbled backward, and — in an unfortunate twist of fate — tripped over a display of plastic-wrapped celery.

Celery, in case you were wondering, is not a particularly forgiving thing to land on.

There was silence. Then...

"Cleanup in produce!" a voice called, entirely too delighted by my misfortune.

A ripple of amusement swept through the shoppers. A few stifled laughs. A muttered, "Did she just take out the cantaloupes?" from a man near the apples.

The store employees appeared as if summoned by incantation, aprons rustling, brooms and dustpans materializing. One young worker, clearly an example of just how far an English degree went these days, chided, "Melon-choly disaster."

I adjusted my glasses, willing my dignity to remain intact. "Quite fine, thank you," I told a young clerk offering to help me up. "Just a little... research gone awry."

Another chuckle from the peanut gallery.

I spotted my chance to escape — a narrow gap between the bagged salads and the bakery. I turned to make my retreat.

"Mother!"

I froze.

There was no mistaking that voice.

Stewart.

My son stood tall, pressed, and utterly disapproving,

his arms crossed in the stance he usually reserved for courtroom cross-examinations. His navy suit remained impeccably unruffled, as though even his irritation had been pre-approved by the firm. His calfskin briefcase sat on the floor beside him.

"What on earth are you doing?" he demanded.

I straightened my cardigan. "Grocery shopping."

He exhaled sharply. "This is exactly what I was talking about."

"Stewart, please," I whispered, acutely aware of our audience.

"Mother," he said, voice lower but no less judgmental, "we discussed this. The prying. The unnecessary dramatics. Do you want to end up in the home?"

I stiffened. There it was.

The threat.

Stewart had long been dangling The Home over my head — a retirement community he insisted was "a vibrant, welcoming place" and I insisted was "one step away from being taxidermied in a rocking chair."

Was it too late to consider putting him up for adoption?

"You wouldn't dare," I said, voice like iron.

"Mother," he said in that calm, lawyerly tone, "don't test me."

A soft ripple of sympathetic laughter ran through the crowd.

"You realize some of my clients spend their entire careers trying to manipulate the system, and somehow *you* — armed with a cantaloupe and a cardigan — still manage to cause more damage?"

"Well, *someone* ought to hold it accountable."

With great dignity, I stepped forward, side-stepping a runaway sweet potato, and adjusted my glasses.

"Let's get you home," Stewart sighed, already steering me toward checkout.

"Ooh! Yes! It's about time I checked my gnome nanny cam—either it's caught the porch thief, or I've accidentally recorded three days of Mr. Braxton speed-walking shirtless at dawn," I declared. "Either way, it's a win-win."

Stewart pinched the bridge of his nose.

We walked toward the parking lot and Stewart's Beemer. He muttered the whole way. I eyed him sidelong. As he opened the car door, I spotted a folder jammed into his briefcase—half-tucked, half-forgotten. A motion stuck out from it. I could just make the case name.

ESTATE OF ROSETTA BIANCHI v. CENTURION ENTERPRISES.

Then, in smaller letters: **Dismissed with prejudice.**

The name, Centurion Enterprises, jangled alarm bells in my head, but I had more pressing things to worry about.

Mildred Jansen's secret companion—a mystery that remained unsolved.

And if Stewart had his way, I was running out of time. But I had a sharp brain—and I had prunes.

CHAPTER TWO

Here's what no one tells you about getting old: *you don't feel old.*

Oh, sure, the knees start sounding like a bag of microwave popcorn when you stand up. The back develops very specific opinions about mattresses. And suddenly, you know way too much about fiber.

But inside?

Inside, you're still the same guy. The same wiseass detective who could drink a pot of coffee and survive a stakeout on nothing but nerves and bad takeout. The same man who didn't think twice about chasing down a perp in a dark alley.

The same man who could, and would, knock the smug right off Roger Whitaker's golf cheating face if given half a chance.

But the world forgets that.

Your family forgets. Your doctor forgets. Hell, the guy at the deli counter starts calling you "young man" in that tone that means the exact opposite.

And before you know it, your own daughter is

threatening to shove you into a retirement home like a broken recliner with a busted lever.

Shady Pines.

The name alone made me want to shove my head in a bucket of denture cream.

So, yeah. I had some thoughts about the whole "growing old gracefully" thing.

But at that particular moment, my biggest problem wasn't my looming exile to the land of lukewarm soup.

It was the fact that Dr. Chuckles had both hands shoved into my mouth like he was fixing a clogged drain.

I sat in the dentist's chair, feeling less like a patient and more like a Buick up on the lift.

The overhead light was bright enough to interrogate war criminals, and Dr. Chuckles — whose real name I had zero interest in remembering — was making himself right at home in my molars.

"Y'know, doc," I mumbled around what felt like an entire Home Depot aisle worth of metal tools, "my family thinks I should be knitting rather than nabbing birdies — or bogeys, as luck would have it."

Dr. Chuckles, who really should have pursued a career in stand-up, waggled his eyebrows as he worked.

"Mmhmm," he hummed — a man of few words when elbow-deep in another man's wisdom teeth.

"Made a swing so wild," I continued, the suction tube slurping like a dying goldfish, "I nearly took out the mayor's poodle. Would've been a real hole-in-one."

I tried to chuckle, but it came out as a garbled, wheezing snort.

Dr. Chuckles grinned. "Keep it up and you're gonna

choke on your own spit."

Suddenly, he made a noise — a cross between a grunt and the sound you make when you open a fridge and something smells *off.*

"Bad news, Hy." He reached for a comically oversized syringe. "You need a root canal, my friend."

Root canal? Oh, Chuckles, you are so not my friend.

I groaned. "You sure? Maybe it just needs a good talking-to."

Dr. Chuckles grinned. "Oh, it's getting a talking-to, all right. Open wide."

Before I could argue, he jabbed me in the gum with enough anesthetic to drop a small horse.

"Well," Dr. Chuckles yelled over the whir of the drill. "I've got my retirement all figured out. No Boca Raton for me. I'm going to live on a cruise ship!"

I raised an eyebrow. "*Cruth thip?*"

Damned novocaine.

"Yep! Travel the world, meet new folks every week. Endless buffets and not a single blade of grass to mow."

I sat up a little straighter. That actually sounded — *good.*

Maybe the trick wasn't fighting the inevitable. *Maybe it was cheating it.*

Dr. Chuckles had a point. Maybe I didn't need to prove I still had gas in the tank.

Maybe I just needed to burn rubber before anyone noticed the check engine light was on.

They wanted me parked. In neutral. Engine cooling.

But I still had fuel to burn — and I wasn't done driving.

The trick to a good stakeout was patience. And prunes.

I had both.

Seated in my well-worn recliner, a cup of tea cooling on the side table, I popped one of those wrinkled bad boys in my mouth and adjusted my binoculars before peering through the slats of my living room blinds.

Across the street, Brenda Calloway was up to her usual tricks — watering her lawn in a tennis skirt that didn't have the real estate to cover her backside.

"Third time today," I murmured. A remarkable devotion to greenery, considering she'd already let three husbands wither on the vine. "What are you hiding, Calloway? Because it's certainly not your derriere."

I lifted my binoculars and zoomed in.

Ah-ha. The mailman.

Again.

My lips pursed. Coincidence? I thought not.

I jotted it down in my notebook, right below "Mr. Braxton jogs suspiciously fast for a man with two hip replacements. Fountain of Youth or stronger prescription than the rest of us?" and "The Petersons' garbage schedule remains an enigma. Either they're testing the limits of waste management, or they've been taking lessons from Poe on how to hide a body."

Some people played bridge. Some took up knitting.

I conducted neighborhood reconnaissance.

And I was very good at it.

Just as I was about to shift my focus to Mrs. O'Leary's peculiar trash schedule, my binoculars went dark.

I jerked back.

Outside my window, blocking my view entirely, stood a six-foot-tall brick wall of disappointment.

Stewart.

I lowered my binoculars slowly, like a criminal caught red-handed.

"Mother," he said. Just that. My name, boiled down to a single syllable of pure judgment.

I gave him my best innocent smile. "Stewart, darling! What a surprise."

He didn't move.

Didn't blink.

"We're going for a drive," he announced.

"Now? Oh, Stewart, I'd love to, but I have very pressing—"

"Now."

And that was how I found myself in a car, against my will, on a one-way trip to my worst nightmare.

Stewart parked in front of Sunnycrest Assisted Living, a name so aggressively cheerful it felt like a trap.

"Just a visit," he said, putting the car in park.

"Just a visit," I repeated, eyeing the building like it might bite.

Stewart got out. I did not.

Then he opened my door.

The betrayal.

I clutched my purse like a woman about to be mugged and stepped into the land of the nearly departed.

Inside, the air smelled like disinfectant and something

18

vaguely peach-scented, the kind of artificial fruitiness that tried to cover up something far less pleasant.

A receptionist with the hollow cheer of a person who'd long since given up on their dreams greeted us with weaponized enthusiasm.

"Oh, Mr. Drye, welcome! And this must be your lovely mother!"

The lovely mother who was about to fake her own death to get out of this.

Stewart smiled in that polished, lawyerly way that meant he was about to sell my soul.

"I'd love to know more about the amenities," he said smoothly. "Mom's considering her options."

I was absolutely not considering my options.

But Stewart and the receptionist began their little sales pitch, so I did what I did best.

I observed.

The "game room" was silent, save for the slow mechanical voice of an old bingo caller.

A group of seniors sat in a circle "playing chess" — on an empty board.

A woman in a rocking chair stared at a wall that had absolutely nothing on it.

A man in an ill-fitting sweater sighed deeply into a bowl of plain oatmeal.

And then I saw *him*.

Old Mr. Farnsworth, a former neighbor, standing at the locked exit door, punching in random codes like a prisoner trying to break out.

A shiver went down my spine.

This wasn't a retirement community.

This was heaven's waiting room.

And Stewart wanted to park me here.

Like an old car, stored away until it eventually rusted. *Not today.*

"Excuse me," I said sweetly, cutting off Stewart mid-sentence. "I need to use the ladies' room."

I shuffled off quickly, turned a corner, and—bolted.

If I had my library sneakers on, I could've made a cleaner getaway, but I had to work with what I had.

I ducked past an orderly, then weaved through a *tai chi* class, which was mostly just people slowly waving their hands.

"Ma'am?" a nurse called behind me. "Do you need assistance finding your room?"

MY ROOM.

I walked faster.

"Come on, Dr. Scholl's. Don't fail me now," I whispered.

A man with a walker tried to engage me in conversation about the war.

"Fascinating, dear," I said, power-walking past him.

The doors. So close.

I was nearly there when—

"Mother!"

I froze.

Stewart stood at the front desk, half-exasperated, half-resigned.

I braced myself. I had one shot. I turned—and ran straight into a magazine rack.

Papers went flying. Brochures scattered.

And that's when I saw it.

My sign.

PHOTURIS CRUISE LINES: SAIL INTO YOUR GOLDEN YEARS.

I snatched up the brochure.

A cruise.

A floating city.

No locked doors. No slow bingo. No beige colored death sentence.

I wouldn't be parked.

I wouldn't be stored away.

I'd sail *away.*

Stewart rushed to my side, followed by the worried administrator, who had "pending lawsuit" emblazoned across her forehead like a tattoo.

Me? I fanned the brochure like it was the second coming of menopause, heart racing with an idea so audacious it almost made me giddy.

Stewart barely glanced at it. "Mother, honestly. Come on. Let's get out of here."

Exactly.

I tucked the pamphlet into my purse, schooling my expression into the very picture of weary resignation.

He thought he was leading me out of here. Thought he'd won.

But I wasn't being led anywhere.

I was plotting my escape.

And for once in my life, I didn't need a Dewey Decimal number to tell me exactly where I was going.

I had a killer *plan.*

CHAPTER THREE

The cruise terminal was a special kind of hell — an unholy fusion of airport security, a cattle call, and senior discount day at the grocery store. The air was thick with sunscreen, cologne, and the unmistakable tang of stress and Viagra.

I adjusted my grip on my duffel, already regretting my life choices.

This was supposed to be relaxing.

Instead, I was stuck in a sluggish line, boxed in by fanny packs, sun visors, and a couple bickering about whether they'd packed enough antacids. I'd survived stakeouts in worse conditions, but this? This was testing my patience.

And then, as if the universe wanted to shove my blood pressure just a little higher, *she* happened.

A woman in a crisp white blazer, designer sunglasses perched atop her perfectly coiffed hair, cut right in front of me like she had diplomatic immunity. No hesitation. No sheepish glance. Just a flick of her wrist as she handed over her documents, breezing past the rest of us poor schmucks like we were merely set dressing.

I let out a slow breath through my nose.

"Unbelievable," I muttered.

She didn't look back.

I debated saying something—really let her know what I thought about people like her—but I decided against it. Not worth the energy. Besides, the last time I called someone out in a line, I ended up on a neighborhood watch list.

I shook my head and shuffled forward, pretending to admire the promotional posters of the ship.

THE PHOTURIS: LUXURY, ADVENTURE, AND UNFORGETTABLE MEMORIES AWAIT!

I had a feeling I'd be making memories, all right. Just not the kind they were advertising.

That's when I spotted *him*.

A jittery guy near the luggage drop, checking his watch like he expected bad news.

Thin. Wiry. Balding at the temples. His foot tapped against the tile, his fingers twitching at his sides like he had too much caffeine or not enough nerve.

And then, under his breath, he muttered something while he smacked his ticket against his hand.

I wouldn't have caught it if I hadn't been stuck two feet away.

"He's gonna know. He's gonna know... he's got to know by now."

That old instinct kicked in, the one that had kept me alive through more than a few bad situations. That wasn't just a nervous traveler. That was someone expecting the axe to fall.

His eyes flicked up and landed on me.

For a split second, we locked eyes.

His face went pale.

And then—just like that—he turned and disappeared into the crowd, swallowed up by the chaos of rolling suitcases and floral shirts.

I frowned, filing it away for later.

Then, just as I shifted forward again—

A deep, big voice, sharp with tension, cut through the noise. "This ship ain't big enough for both of us, Reggie."

I turned my head just in time to see a friendly handshake that was missing the friendly.

"I mean it, Bart."

One guy was thin, balding, his polo shirt a little too crisp. Reggie Bart, I guessed. He looked sort of familiar—maybe I bowled against him?

The other was built like a retired linebacker, squeezed into a Hawaiian shirt that barely contained him.

The big guy had his fingers locked around the other man's hand, the kind of grip that was meant to prove a point.

Not a hello. A warning.

The fellow named Bart tried to pull back, but the big guy held on a beat too long, his jaw clenching.

I didn't catch what the first guy said—if he even responded.

But I saw the flicker of something in his eyes—something I'd seen a million times. Didn't matter if it was in the face of a victim or a perp. It looked the same.

Fear.

Not the kind you get when you suddenly remember you forgot your anniversary. Nah. It was the kind that meant this wasn't over yet.

Bart yanked his hand away. His ring clunked against the gangway rail. He straightened, adjusted his collar, and walked off without another word.

The big guy watched him go, shaking his head before turning away.

I scratched my chin.

A nervous guy muttering about somebody knowing something. A not so friendly handshake with a veiled threat.

And we hadn't even boarded yet.

I sighed, adjusting my bag and stepping forward in line.

Then — just as I reached the boarding gate — I hesitated. Not for the mystery. Not for the weird feeling in my gut.

For Gloria.

She didn't know I was doing this.

I told myself it was easier this way. That I'd call her when we reached the first port, let her know I was fine, let her yell at me for running off without so much as a "Hey, kid, guess what your old man did."

But right now? If I called, she'd drop her shrimp mold and drive straight down here to drag me home.

Only… home wasn't the same anymore.

She had her husband. The kids. The whole life she built after her mother died. And I was… what? A relic? A piece of furniture that didn't quite fit in the living room anymore?

No. I shook off the doubt. This was the right decision.

I wasn't dead yet. And I'd be damned if I was gonna sit around waiting for that moment to sneak up on me.

I took one last breath of land air, squared my shoulders, and stepped forward onto the gangway.

This was the start of the rest of my life.

I thought about the twitchy bald guy, the Hawaiian Hulk, and the naggingly familiar man in the polo shirt.

So, why was my gut telling me it might just wind up being the end of someone else's?

***

The ship's horn let out a low, majestic groan — less foghorn, more freedom cry — and I swear I felt it vibrate through my sternum like a second heartbeat. It startled a flock of seagulls and two grown men clutching Bloody Marys, but I just closed my eyes and smiled.

Goodbye to Stewart's gentle sighs and calendar reminders to "just relax."

Goodbye to the neighbors who paused at the end of my driveway, deciding if a wave might invite a conversation about property taxes or the sudden disappearance of their garden gnome.

Goodbye to being the woman people whispered about — not for scandal, but for being *interested.*

The *Photuris* slipped its leash and drifted from the dock with theatrical grace, and I stood at the railing in my sensible but chic shoes, a wide-brimmed hat anchored against the breeze, and a fresh notebook, crisp pages waiting, in my tote.

No casserole rotas. No HOA agendas. Just SPF 70 and open water.

Let the watching — and the wondering — begin.

I stepped onto the Lido Deck like a Victorian botanist stumbling upon an undiscovered species of spring break. The humidity hit me first — thick, warm, and vaguely pineapple-scented. Then came the sounds: steel drum covers of '80s power ballads — was that Whitesnake's "Here I Go Again" — a lifeguard's whistle slicing the air like punctuation, and the unmistakable clatter of someone dropping a full plate of nachos.

The décor was a riot of saturated optimism — aquamarine tile, coral-print lounge cushions, and more fake bamboo than a tiki bar on half-price night. The ceiling fans turned lazily overhead, doing absolutely nothing for the heat but looking festive while failing.

A man in a tank top that read *"Call Me Big Kahuna"* was bellowing at the bartender like he was summoning a genie. "Make it a double! Again!" he crowed, raising his cup like he'd just secured a small nation.

I slid to the side of the walkway, pulled my notebook from my tote, and did what any self-respecting retired librarian with a fascination for human behavior would do.

I documented.

Subject 1: *Woman wrestling a flamingo-shaped pool float. Possibly a bachelorette. Probably a Guest Injury Form soon to be filed by the Safety Officer.*

Subject 2: *Shirtless man with spray tan and Bluetooth headset arguing with someone about "NFT tax shelters."*

Subject 3: *Child with a popsicle, unattended. Possible future pickpocket. Sticky. Highly mobile.*

I jotted quickly, ducked behind a faux palm tree, and let the scene wash over me.

It was part circus, part fever dream, and one hundred percent a goldmine of mischief, motives, and misbehavior.

In short: *heaven.*

Before I could properly judge the shrimp on the buffet — languishing under a pink heat lamp like they were about to be grilled on their whereabouts the night of April 7 — a young woman materialized at my side like a hospitality fairy godmother.

Her uniform was standard cruise fare: navy polo, name tag, a logo that looked vaguely like a sun doing jazz hands.

Fosse, Fosse, Fosse…

But she wore it like a badge of honor. Her bun was military-tight, her shoes squeaked just slightly, and her smile… oh, her smile. It was the kind that said, *"I will absolutely find you a clean towel or hide a body for you, depending on which you need first."*

She held out a drink the color of a Lisa Frank folder. "Welcome aboard, ma'am," she said, handing it to me like it was peace in a plastic cup. "Let me know if you need anything."

I took it carefully. It was sweating more than the tourists.

"Now that you mention it, I may need an extra straw and something intriguing to wrap my little gray cells around," I said.

She blinked, then smiled wider — genuine this time, not service standard. "Well, we do have trivia night in the lounge. General knowledge. No wagering. Gets a little competitive."

"A little competition keeps the blood flowing."

"And the blood flowing keeps the liability waivers signed," she added dryly.

I liked her immediately.

Her name tag read Laila, and there was something about her — something behind the calm poise and cruise-approved script — that made me pause. Her eyes were warm, but they held just the faintest edge of weariness. Not exhaustion. Something older. Familiar.

I took a sip. Coconut. Grenadine. Rum that could strip varnish.

It was, in a word, perfect.

"Thank you, Laila," I said, with all the weight of someone who hadn't been offered kindness without strings in a long time.

She nodded once, then turned to answer a call from someone shouting *"SWEETHEART!"* like it was her legal name.

And just like that, the spell was broken.

I placed a gentle hand on her arm. "Don't you let that awful cretin demean you like that. Your worth is greater than that."

"Thank you." She smiled gratefully, then sighed. "Unfortunately, it comes with the territory. Please, enjoy your cruise."

I kept a keen eye on her as she walked away to tend to the belligerent guest, tucking her name away in my notes, right under **Subject 4:** *One to Watch.*

Not because I thought she'd done anything wrong.

But because my gut told me that sooner or later, something would be done to *her*. And I don't much like watching good girls fall without someone asking the right questions.

I was just about to slip my travel diary back into my tote when a new presence joined the conversation—thin, balding, with a polo shirt so neatly pressed it almost seemed smug. For a fleeting moment, I wondered if he shopped at the same store as Stewart.

His shoes gleamed like he'd paid someone to scuff them just enough to look casual. Not handsome, exactly, but practiced. Like someone who wanted to be recognized, though I couldn't yet recall for what.

He gave me a glance—passing, dismissive—and then locked eyes on Laila.

"How about something sweet from the bar, doll—unless, of course, you're on the menu." His veneers gleamed almost as bright as the diamond in his ostentatious pinkie ring.

At any rate, his words fell flat, like a pancake pretending to be a soufflé. Laila flinched—just for a moment. Blink-and-you-miss-it—but I didn't blink.

"Charge it to cabin 9274. Bart," he ordered.

She offered a nod so polished it could've been policy, and turned away, already disappearing into the blur of poolside bustle.

The man watched her go, no shame, no second thought. He adjusted his cuff, took out his phone, and started scrolling—like nothing had happened.

I studied him.

Not out of outrage, though heaven knew I'd filed a few patron complaints in my day. No — this was different. There was something under his skin, a tightness in his jaw, an edge behind the ease.

And something else.

Recognition, maybe? Not quite. But a whisper of it. A face I'd seen somewhere — perhaps above a caption in the business section or the byline of an editorial with too many commas and not enough soul.

I tapped a line into my notebook:

Subject 5: *Bart. Cabin 9274. Sharp shirt. Sharper tongue. Possibly familiar. Observe.*

Because men like that? They didn't always get caught doing something wrong.

But they usually *did something worth catching.*

That's when I spotted him.

Subject 6: *The Hawaiian Hulk.*

Not so much pacing as prowling, like a jungle cat stuffed into Tommy Bahama and barely tolerating the dress code. His shirt — aggressively tropical — was straining across a chest you could bounce quarters off of, assuming you had a strong throwing arm and a last will and testament.

He wasn't sightseeing. He was watching. Calculating.

The kind of man who didn't just size people up — he weighed them. Morally. Strategically. Like he'd once decided whether someone lived or limped away from a boardroom.

He passed by with a grunt that sounded like it had legal consequences. Didn't look at me. Didn't need to.

I eased behind a decorative potted palm and made a note:

Subject 6: *Built like an Amana side-by-side. Possibly corporate muscle. Avoid eye contact. Possibly also sugar.*

Something about him made the hairs on the back of my neck rise like they'd heard a rumor I hadn't.

That's when I realized I wasn't the only one taking notes.

Across the Lido Deck, leaning against a deck chair as though he didn't trust it not to collapse, stood a man with storm-gray eyebrows, a tactical stance, and the energy of a man who'd once interrogated a suspect with nothing but a cup of black coffee and a phonebook.

He wasn't watching the pool games or the daiquiri line. He was watching people. Closely. Quietly. And not just for fun.

He clocked the man in the crisp polo. Then, seconds later, the walking kitchen appliance in the Magnum P.I. dad wear.

He wasn't just browsing. He was connecting dots.

I felt a flicker of admiration.

I knew that look.

I'd worn that look.

It said: *"One of you is going to make this vacation interesting, and I'm going to find out who first."*

A fellow pattern-watcher. Possibly a former professional. Definitely not here for the bingo.

I made a note.

Subject 6½: *Silver fox. Watchful. Possibly ex-law enforcement. Possibly trouble. Also, possibly my new favorite person aboard.*

Then he turned and looked straight at me.

Not past me. Not through me.

At me.

His expression didn't change, but I saw the flicker of recognition, or more likely, assessment. Like he'd just realized *I* was connecting the same dots.

For a heartbeat, we were two magnets circling each other's polarity.

Then his eyes dipped, just a breath too long, to my sunhat, my notebook, and my shoes, which were *perfectly* sensible *and* purchased fifty percent off.

And just like that, the flicker snuffed itself out.

I added a line.

Or not.

I'd just finished scribbling when *she* appeared. She wafted by like a breeze that didn't touch anyone else.

Subject 7: *Lady in White.*

Not "wearing" white. *Inhabiting* it. Crisp, creaseless linen. Diamond studs that probably had names. Sunglasses that hid a thousand daggers and a walk like she was floating one inch above the rest of us out of sheer disdain.

She glided past the loungers and inflatable pool chaos like it was all beneath her, which, to be fair, it probably was.

Her hair was perfect. Her posture was a weapon. And her eyes? Locked on *him.*

The man in the polo.

Her gaze didn't waver, didn't blink. Not a glance of recognition. No rage. Just *focus.*

There was something in the muscle working beneath

those razor-sharp cheekbones, in the way she gripped the strap of her handbag with fingers just this side of white-knuckled, that told me whatever was going through her mind, she'd rehearsed it. And that this was *not* their first encounter.

I made a note.

Subject 7: *Definitely planning something. Hoping it's legal. Betting it's not.*

And if it wasn't?

I had a feeling I'd be there when the plan unfolded. Preferably with a front-row seat and something bubbly.

Just as I was about to commit to judging the ice sculpture—swan or melted otter, still pending—I heard it.

A scream. A real one.

Not the "I dropped my cocktail" kind.

Not the "my child just cannonballed into my mimosa" kind.

No, this was raw. Ripped from the gut. And instantly, every hair on my arms stood at attention like a battalion of tiny soldiers.

I dropped my drink.

The little paper umbrella spun away like a tragic ballerina, landing belly-up in a puddle of rum. My notebook slid half out of my tote, its spine catching the light like it, too, had perked up at the scent of mystery.

I turned toward the source of the sound.

People were already moving. Some rushed forward. Others inched back. All of them buzzed like startled bees.

Then I saw Laila—wide-eyed and shaking—hand pressed to her mouth, standing beside a lounge chair frozen.

And in the chair?

A man.

The man.

Hey, doll. Crisp polo. Now rumpled. Mouth slack. Sunglasses askew.

One hand still clutching a half-finished Bourbon Cherry Bomb, the other resting against his stomach in a gesture that looked eerily like he'd just realized something was very, very wrong. And something was very, very wrong.

He wasn't moving.

I stepped forward instinctively, years of library incident report filing and human behavior analysis clicking into place like well-worn dominoes. I leaned over, tuchus unabashedly sticking out behind me, staring at the scene like it was one of those Magic Eye pictures.

And that's when I realized I wasn't the only one approaching.

He was too.

Storm-gray eyebrows. Tactical posture. A duffel still slung over one shoulder.

He stopped right next to me. We stared down at the very dead man. Then at each other.

"Nobody touch anything," he said, voice like gravel and judgment.

I arched a brow. "Then kindly remove your ham hand from my keister."

He blinked.

I didn't.

He carefully removed his hand, which had

inadvertently been resting on my backside. And just like that, the game was afoot.

CHAPTER FOUR

The guy in the crisp polo was still slouched like a man trying to nap through his own funeral — that, or his wife's bridge night. Legs splayed. Sunglasses crooked. One hand hanging off the lounger as if it had just given up halfway through a toast.

The med crew arrived suspiciously fast. Too fast. Almost as though they'd been waiting just offstage for their cue.

They gave him the once-over. A quick check at the neck. A two-finger prod at the wrist. One of them leaned in, and I waited for him to say something meaningful, but all he did was nod to the other, like, *Yep. Toasted.*

"Unfortunate incident," the lead guy said, tugging off his gloves. He may as well have just finished potting petunias. "Heatstroke, most likely."

Heatstroke, my ass.

I'd seen teenagers fake worse to avoid gym class. And perps? They could flop like soccer stars if it meant skipping arraignment. But this? This didn't feel like performance art or poor hydration. This felt planned, and not by him.

The guy's drink was still on the little plastic table beside him, barely touched. Bourbon Cherry Bomb. Sweet. Cold. *Deadly?*

A woman to my left gasped into her sunhat. A man with an ironic mustache muttered something about travel insurance. The deck rippled with whispers. Gossip in a church pew.

The captain arrived ten minutes too late and five excuses too polished. Captain Montague "Monty" Harrigan.

Captain Monty looked like he'd been poured into his uniform by a PR team. White jacket, gold trim, a smile so practiced it probably had rehearsal notes. He had the kind of tan that said *I work on a ship but haven't touched saltwater in a decade,* and the way he strutted onto the deck made me wonder if he thought the national anthem played every time he entered a room.

"Folks, folks. Let's settle down. Now, I realize this is an unfortunate situation…"

Pretty unfortunate for the dead guy.

"…we believe it was heat exhaustion," he announced to the small crowd, straightening his jacket like that made it official. "The Caribbean sun can be quite unforgiving."

Unforgiving, sure. But not usually fatal in under ten sips of bourbon. Not to mention, I don't think The Keys counted as "the Caribbean." We'd hardly hit international waters yet.

I narrowed my eyes and folded my arms. Something stank, and it wasn't the shrimp buffet.

This wasn't the kind of death you shrugged off with a cold towel and a complimentary mimosa.

They rolled the body away on a gurney draped in pool towels — the kind with cartoon crabs doing the cha-cha — as if a little terrycloth dignity could patch over the fact that someone had just died mid-happy hour. The crowd scattered, murmuring in the uneasy way people do when their vacation gets bumped off script. A few looked genuinely rattled. Most just looked annoyed they'd missed their turn in the conga line.

Then there was the busybody.

She was scribbling away in a small notebook, bright eyes darting around the scene. Probably a bored housewife who'd watched one too many episodes of *Murder, She Wrote.*

I needed caffeine and clarity, not necessarily in that order.

The nearest coffee station was one of those sad little kiosks with fake wood paneling and a tip jar that read **Life's too short for bad coffee,** which felt, frankly, too on-the-nose for the moment. I braced for the inevitable. A weak brew, burned aftertaste, and a barista whose soul had long since abandoned ship.

Still, old habits die hard — and caffeine was my coping mechanism of choice.

I took my cup and leaned against the rail nearby, letting the sting of cheap java chase the aftertaste of suspicion. I didn't like the way that had gone down. Too fast. Too tidy. Too many nods and not enough questions.

That's when I felt the presence. Not subtle. Not soft. More like a question mark in orthopedic wedges.

"Lovely day for heatstroke," she said, her voice like lemon zest. Sharp, bright, and hard to ignore.

I didn't have to turn to know who it was.

"Next, we'll be offering complimentary CPR with every umbrella drink."

He glanced sideways. "Bourbon Cherry Bomb," he muttered.

"Hardly a refreshing choice," she replied.

"Wasn't for him," I grunted. I cleared my throat. "By the way, I'm, uh, sorry about that whole hand thing."

"Consider it forgotten. Just don't let it become a habit." She smiled slightly.

"Wouldn't dream of it," I snorted. She looked a little offended at that.

Women. One of life's mysteries I may never solve.

I decided to change the subject. "So, you buying what the good captain's selling?"

She didn't answer right away. Just stepped up beside me, her own cup in hand, steam curling between us like a tentative handshake.

"Not particularly. And I don't like it when people lie," she said eventually. "Especially with pool toys nearby. Sets a bad example for the younger generation."

I nodded. "Heatstroke, huh?"

"Hmm," she hummed, noncommittal. But her eyes were already scanning, flicking from the now-empty lounge chair to the damp circle where the spilled cocktail had stained the deck. A crime scene with garnish.

"Name's Hy," I offered. "Hy Reynolds."

"Eugenia Drye," she said. "Retired librarian. Unretired troublemaker."

I chuckled. "Retired detective. Same résumé."

We stood like that for a moment, watching the crew mop the chaos into neatness. Just two seniors sipping subpar coffee, already cataloging inconsistencies.

Retirement, my keister. We were just getting started.

***

I'd seen plenty of dramatic moments in my day. Committee implosions, holiday potlucks gone rogue. Even the great PTA blowout of 2007, when Beverly Cranston used laxatives in her congratulatory chocolate cupcakes to get back at Marla Frank for stealing the president's seat. But nothing quite like this.

The man was dead. Stone-cold. Not in the fainting-couch, *oh heavens, I need a damp cloth* sort of way, but in the slack-jawed, soul-has-left-the-building fashion that required more than Gatorade and a breezy hat.

And yet, there they were, rolling him off with all the ceremony of a sunburned guest who'd had one too many. A few towels artfully draped, a couple of hushed phrases into walkie-talkies, and poof! Tragedy, sanitized and swept aside like it might delay the limbo contest.

"Heatstroke," someone whispered behind me, as though the word itself carried antiseptic powers.

Heatstroke. Please.

I'd seen enough genuine emergencies to know when something didn't add up, and this had subtraction written all over it. The man's drink hadn't spilled until after he slumped. His sunglasses were still clinging to one ear. And his color? No amount of Caribbean sun did *that* to a man's complexion.

No, this wasn't some unlucky brush with tropical dehydration.

This was curated. Packaged. Presented to the masses with just enough plausible deniability to let the shrimp cocktail resume its spotlight.

"Heatstroke," I muttered under my breath. "Is the new *ignore this and get back to bingo.*"

But I wasn't quite ready to pick up my dauber and move on.

Not yet.

They'd barely wheeled him away, gurney swaddled in pool towels like some tragic spa burrito, before the cleaning crew descended. Three of them. Rubber gloves, grim expressions, and a bottle of cleanser that could probably dissolve guilt.

They scrubbed the lounger with the intensity of a Silkwood shower.

But I wasn't watching them. Not really.

I was watching what he'd left behind.

The cocktail glass. It rested innocuously on the nearby table, upended so the ruddy liquid spilled across the surface of the table. The ice tinkled against the glass as it shifted, melting in the overhead sun. Umbrella still perched at a jaunty angle. Cherry rolling back and forth in the sea breeze.

It looked almost festive. If you ignored the corpse.

I narrowed my eyes.

Bourbon Cherry Bomb.

I'd tasted one years ago at a retirement gala that turned into a polka conga line and two annulments. Not mine, but I could give names.

I tried to remember the taste. Too sweet, barely any kick. Unless someone added their own. Something bitter. Something permanent.

Curious. Very curious.

I made a mental note to investigate the ingredients and who might've slipped in a final twist. Because whatever killed him, it wasn't the sun.

I scanned the crowd the way I used to scan overdue checkout slips. Calmly, methodically, and fully prepared to issue a fine. Most people were already peeling away, eager to return to their pool chairs and bottomless Mai Tais, pretending they hadn't just witnessed a man expire mid-cocktail.

Grief? Hardly. Shock? Not convincing. But interest? *That was alive and kicking.*

The woman in white—cool, poised, and sculpted like vengeance in linen—watched Captain Monty with narrowed eyes. Not frightened. Focused. Then she vanished into the crowd like Jeannie C. Riley's "Harper Valley PTA."

The man in the aggressively tropical shirt lingered longer than necessary, arms crossed, expression unreadable. His gaze swept the deck like he was running threat assessments instead of vacationing.

And then... the one from the pool. Older. Grizzled. *Ham hands.*

He stood apart. Not in mourning, not in panic, but observation. Eyes sharp. Shoulders squared. The way cops look when they're not wearing a badge anymore, but haven't stopped carrying the weight of one.

He noticed everything. Including me.

So, I gave him the smallest nod.

He didn't return it. But he didn't look away either.

I flipped open my notebook, shielding it casually behind the brim of my hat, and scribbled:

Subject 6 ½: *Watchful. Almost certainly retired law enforcement. Equal parts cynicism and cholesterol. Monitor.*

I sauntered over to the coffee station. He stood there like someone had parked him. Sturdy. Silent. Irritated by the very existence of non-black coffee.

He grunted.

I offered a polite smile, the kind I reserved for misbehaving library patrons and poorly written municipal bylaws.

"Lovely day for heatstroke," I ventured. "Next, we'll be offering complimentary CPR with every umbrella drink."

The man glanced sideways. "Bourbon Cherry Bomb," he muttered.

Hm. He'd noted the drink.

"Hardly a refreshing choice," I replied, stirring my own cup.

"Definitely wasn't for him," he grunted.

He fumbled through some semblance of an apology for fondling my rear. If you want to know the truth, it was the most action I'd seen since my husband died ten years ago. So, of course I was a little put out when he made it crystal clear it wouldn't be happening again.

"Hy," he said after we briefly discussed the validity of the captain's proclamation. He stuck out a hand. "Hy Reynolds."

"Eugenia Drye," I replied. "Retired librarian. Unretired troublemaker."

That earned me the tiniest smirk—more eyebrow twitch than expression—but I considered it a win.

As he looked back toward the deck, I casually slipped my notebook from my tote and scribbled.

Subject 6½: *Hy Reynolds. Retired detective confirmed. Definitely skeptical. Do not offer him flavored creamer. Do ask later what he noticed that I missed.*

He didn't seem to mind the scribbling. Or maybe he did and just assumed I'd do it anyway.

Smart man.

CHAPTER FIVE

I didn't trust anyone who whistled before coffee, which made about half the breakfast buffet immediate suspects.

The sun had barely cleared the lifeboats and already people were lined up like cattle at a Vegas trough, loading their plates with enough pancakes and pork product to put a cardiologist on speed dial. I grabbed a tray, made a show of piling on bacon, and kept my eyes peeled.

This wasn't about breakfast. It was about behavior.

I scanned the line, cataloging reactions like I used to catalog priors. A couple in matching **Cruise Hair, Don't Care** shirts giggled over the waffle bar like a man hadn't dropped dead twenty feet from the shrimp station yesterday. Business as usual.

A woman near the fruit display dabbed her eyes with a napkin, though she didn't look particularly sad. More like she was practicing for an audition on a soap no one watched anymore. Performance.

The buffet line shuffled along. I wrinkled my nose. The ham looked criminal — glazed within an inch of its life and sweating like a felon on the stand — but I kept my focus on the man standing next to it.

Tom Selleck on steroids.

He wasn't in line for food. Wasn't looking around, either. Just standing there by the carving station, glaring at the steam trays. One hand in his pocket, the other clutched around a phone he was muttering into.

"I told him not to push it," he said, low and clipped.

I ladled the redeye gravy, pretending I was focused, but I was listening.

"No, I didn't sign anything," he added, voice sharper now.

A pause. I watched him fish a handkerchief from his pocket and wipe the damp sheen of sweat gathering on his forehead.

"I'm not going down for this."

My ears perked. Not exactly the kind of thing you say after a friendly business brunch.

He must've felt the weight of my gaze — or maybe my bacon camouflage wasn't as subtle as I thought — because he turned.

Our eyes met.

For a second, I thought he was going to launch a pineapple at me.

Instead, he gave a tight nod that felt more like a warning than a greeting, tucked the phone back into his pocket, and stalked off toward the juice bar.

I watched him go, then returned to my tray.

Didn't matter how much gravy I poured.

Everything still tasted like motive.

I added three scoops of eggs I didn't want and averted my gaze.

I'd just snagged a fresh cup of coffee — hotter than the surface of the sun and twice as bitter — when I caught sight of her again, the Lady in White. Still dressed like she'd ordered the "Botox blank" look straight from a catalog. And yet, somehow, she still managed to look annoyed.

She was off to the side, near the juice station, hissing something at a man who looked like he belonged to the ship's legal department or maybe a particularly sleazy timeshare office. The kind of guy who says "technically" a lot and means "don't ask."

I wasn't close enough to hear the whole thing, but I caught the tail end.

"…he was about to cut me out of everything. If that prenup held, I'd be lucky to keep the dog."

The guy mumbled something, head bobbing like a dashboard bobblehead. She shook her head, clipped, and walked off like she hadn't just dropped a live wire.

I sipped my coffee, ignoring the fact it was scalding my tongue, and watched her go.

She wasn't mourning anyone. She was managing damage.

No names had been spoken. No context. But if someone was sweating about prenups and proof this early in the cruise? That wasn't small talk. That was motive trying to hide behind a mimosa.

I made a mental note: *Lady in White — sharp tongue, sharper agenda. Possibly lawyering up. Watch her.*

Bart's death had left a mark. Not on the ship's itinerary, apparently, but on the people. You just had to know where to look.

Most people were already pushing it to the back of their minds. Tragedy had a short shelf life when it threatened to interfere with your unlimited mimosa package.

But me? I had questions.

And one of them was standing three feet ahead of me in line, piling blueberries on her French toast like she was fueling up for a stakeout.

Eugenia Drye.

I didn't know what she was up to yet, but I'd bet my last link of sausage, it wasn't just breakfast.

***

I stacked a modest square of French toast on my tray and ladled blueberries over it with academic precision. Blueberries were rich in antioxidants and quite good for the memory, or so the *Reader's Digest* claimed in an issue I'd clipped sometime around 2014. They weren't prunes, but they had their benefits.

I was just about to reach for a dab of whipped cream — life is short, and my cholesterol was just fine and dandy — when I noticed him again.

Hy Reynolds, making his way toward a corner table, permanent scowl firmly in place. His plate was a crime scene of sodium and saturated fats. Three types of meat, all beige, stacked like he was building a bacon-based Tower of Babel.

"Good grief," I muttered under my breath. "He's going to need blueberries." I ladled some extras onto my plate.

I was just returning the stainless-steel ladle when a soft voice spoke beside me.

"Mrs. Drye?"

I turned to find Laila standing there, clipboard in hand, expression caught somewhere between poise and worry. Her bun was still perfectly in place, but her eyes looked a little less rested than the day before.

"Just wanted to check in. I hope you're having a good cruise so far... well, aside from the... you know." She gave a half-smile and gestured vaguely in the direction of the pool deck, as though she could wave away yesterday's corpse like a stray beach ball.

"It's been lovely," I replied. "And you've handled everything with true grace."

She shook her head. "No, really. I wanted to thank you. For yesterday. When Mr. Bart was being..." she trailed off, the name landing like a bruise. "...rude. He could be... difficult. Not everyone would've said something."

I touched her arm gently. "And not everyone has such a high tolerance for condescending men in skin-tight polo shirts. You handled yourself just fine."

Laila offered a grateful smile. "Still. Thank you."

Then she hesitated, glancing down at her clipboard, as if unsure whether to say more. "He seemed perfectly fine when I brought him his drink," she said, almost to herself. "But I've read that heatstroke can come on really suddenly. Especially when you're drinking alcohol.

Sometimes, it just... hits."

I nodded slowly, the words sliding into my mind like a bookmark tucked between pages.

"I suppose it does," I said softly.

She gave me a final polite nod, then turned and headed toward a couple demanding gluten-free pancakes from a man wielding a spatula and the patience of a saint.

I watched her go, balancing my tray to keep the blueberries from rolling.

Laila's words were innocent. Casual. But they weren't forgettable.

Not to a librarian.

I had just enough spring in my step to consider myself sprightly, but not enough to dodge the leg of a deck chair that stuck out like a sore thumb with a vendetta. My foot clipped it. My tray pitched. And in an instant, a small avalanche of blueberries launched into the air like fruity little cannonballs.

They had no sense of direction, just blind ambition.

Several landed with damp plunks along the teak deck. One nestled itself into the cuff of my cardigan like a plum, round hitchhiker. But the rest? Oh, the rest struck dead center on a pristine white linen blouse with all the grace and subtlety of a Jackson Pollock tantrum.

The dollop of whipped cream splatted like an ultimate insult on the Cupid's bow of a very stern, crimson lip.

"Good heavens," I breathed, steadying my plate and stepping forward. "I am so sorry. Please, do let me pay for the dry cleaning. Eugenia Drye. Cabin 9412. I insist. Miss..."

I looked up. The Lady in White. She didn't respond immediately. She looked down at the violet splotches blooming across her bodice. Her expression didn't shift. No horror. No fury. Just a cold, quiet assessment, as though the blueberries had done exactly what she expected of them.

When her eyes met mine, they were the color of overcast skies before a storm. Not wild, or unhinged. Just controlled. Coiled.

"Mrs.," she corrected as I handed her a napkin and she dabbed at the offensive whipped cream. Her bracelet, silver and red, jingled. It seemed slightly incongruous with the rest of her designer ensemble. "Mrs. Alicia Bart," she stated, each syllable shaped with surgical precision.

My throat tightened.

Bart.

As in Bart-the-Body. Bart of the Bourbon Cherry Bomb. Bart, whose sudden case of "heatstroke" had caused such a flurry of towel-draped theatrics just yesterday.

"Oh," I said, keeping my voice light, almost breezy. I pulled my free hand to my chest. "Oh, my. Any... relation?"

"Husband. Not that I would deign to touch the man ever again."

Okay. A little abrupt, but grief worked in funny ways.

"Of course. My... condolences."

She gave a brief nod — imperceptibly shallow. The napkin I had handed her may as well have been a tissue tackling an oil spill. It only smeared the juice the same way it had smeared her bright red lipstick.

Ah, well. It's the thought that counts, right?

Then, just as I opened my mouth to offer another apology or at least an explanation for my blueberry trajectory, she turned and walked away, shoulders back, jaw tight, red-soled heels clicking with the purpose of a woman who'd decided long ago never to appear rattled in public.

She left behind a ghost of citrus and a deeper note — smoky, honeyed wood with a whisper of heat.

I slid my notebook from my tote and scribbled quickly: *Alicia Bart. Estranged? Clearly not devastated. Reaction to the berry assault: clinical. Curious juxtaposition of red against her signature white. Bracelet, shoes, and lips. Clean palette with predatory accents. Do not underestimate.*

I took one last look at the naked French toast on my tray, set it on a side table with a sigh, and made my way toward Hy.

He was sitting at the edge of the dining terrace with his bacon tower, eyes on everything except what was in front of him. Which meant, of course, he saw it all.

I had a few things to tell him. And one or two I planned to keep to myself.

CHAPTER SIX

Eugenia sat down across from me with the kind of precision usually reserved for military drills or high-stakes bridge tournaments. She didn't ask if the seat was taken. Just claimed it like she'd already done the paperwork.

I stabbed a sausage. She eyed the tower of bacon on my plate.

"Wanna guess who the blueberry bombshell is?" she said, reaching for the sugar.

I'd seen her collide with the woman in white like a one-woman fruit salad. "The lady with the linen glare and zero reaction time?"

Eugenia nodded. "She prefers *Mrs.* Alicia Bart."

I paused mid-chew. "As in…"

"As in Bourbon-Cherry-Body-in-the-Chair-Bart."

I whistled through my teeth. "Wife of the deceased. That moves her from 'icy' to 'interesting.'"

"Icy or not, she didn't exactly melt at the mention of his name," Eugenia said, stirring her coffee with clinical calm. "I introduced myself. Offered to pay for the dry cleaning. She offered me a death stare and a name that landed like a gavel."

I sat back, watching Eugenia stare into her coffee as if it were going to cough up an answer. "Spouse is a decent bet. Emotional motive, financial motive, opportunity..."

"She mentioned something, actually. Sounded like she was about to get iced out. Said she'd be lucky to keep the dog."

"Sounds like that lipstick she's sporting might not have been the only red she was seeing."

Eugenia cracked a smile. "Well, she didn't seem particularly bereft. Then again, grief doesn't always show up on schedule. Brenda Calloway sobbed her way through three funerals and still managed to remarry before the casseroles cooled."

I grunted. "Remind me not to accept baked goods from Brenda."

We both looked out across the Lido Deck denizens — families reapplying sunscreen, retirees jostling for shade. Just another morning at sea, if you ignored the corpse from yesterday.

She leaned forward, dropped her voice. "So, what's our play?"

I didn't hesitate. "You've got your notebook. I've got instincts and a hunch that says this wasn't heatstroke."

She nodded once, businesslike. "Then I'd say it's time we made ourselves useful."

We didn't say another word. Just rose together and moved.

Two pensioners with a purpose.

Let the cruise take care of the shuffleboard. We were

chasing something a lot slipperier than pucks.

We took the long way around the upper deck, trying to look casual. Just two retirees on a morning constitutional, if anyone was watching. The sun was already hot enough to fry an egg on the handrails, and the breeze carried that familiar cocktail of sea air, chlorine, and a buffet warming tray left too long in the sun. I squinted against the glare bouncing off every overpriced pair of sunglasses in sight and fought the urge to scratch the spot between my shoulder blades where the back of my shirt was already sticking.

I was just about to make a snide remark about shuffleboard when I saw him.

The guy from the terminal. Twitchy.

Same blazer. Same retreating hairline. Only this time, he wasn't muttering to himself like he was about to flunk a lie detector. He was leaning in toward Captain Monty, talking low and fast.

I heard the sound of paper rustling beside me. Eugenia's face was pinched in consternation as she thumbed furiously through the pages of her notebook.

"Nope." She licked a knotty finger and turned a page. "Nope." Another and another. "Nope, nope. Dang it all. He's not on my list." She immediately began to scribble.

I craned my neck to see.

Subject 8.

"Don't feel bad," I offered. "It takes years of experience to do this job right. And even then—"

Her wrinkled lips puckered in a way that told me I'd better shut up. I turned back toward Twitchy. Potential murderers were safer than angry women.

Twitchy was still standing near one of the crew-access doors, talking to Captain Monty. Scratch that—*pleading* with Monty. His posture was hunched forward. His arms were tense at his sides. Whatever poker face the captain usually wore had cracked wide open. His arms were crossed, his mouth a tight, nervous line. Not angry. *Worried.*

Interesting.

I slowed my pace a fraction, pretending to study a decorative potted palm.

His voice wasn't carrying much, but his body language was practically shouting. He kept glancing around, agitated, like he was afraid someone might overhear, or like someone might already be listening.

"Friend of yours?" Eugenia murmured beside me, her tone light but her eyebrows arched.

"Not exactly," I said. "Saw him yesterday. Twitched his way through the terminal. Definitely a candidate for decaf."

"Not much calmer now," she noted.

"Nope. And the captain's not loving whatever he's hearing."

Twitchy suddenly stepped back, rubbed his hands down his blazer like he'd just remembered what sweat was. "Just don't let anyone see the body," Twitchy said.

Eugenia took a step back. I felt her eyes slide toward mine.

"That's a curious thing to say," she murmured.

I grunted. "Unless he's worried about someone noticing something that doesn't line up with 'heatstroke.'"

"Exactly."

Twitchy turned on his heel and disappeared through the side access door. Monty lingered for a second longer, then followed.

The sea air swirled around us again, a little too warm and sweet. It smelled like sunscreen, secrets, and desperation.

I narrowed my eyes.

"Big boat," I muttered.

"Bigger secrets," Eugenia replied, already scribbling something in that little notebook of hers.

Damned woman was growing on me.

***

The moment Captain Monty and Mr. Blazer vanished into the crew access corridor, I exhaled. Not a gasp. Not a sigh. Just enough to release the knot that had wrapped itself somewhere between my shoulder blades and my better judgment.

The tension they left behind hovered in the air like cheap perfume—insistent, synthetic, and absolutely trying too hard to cover something sour.

I pulled my notebook from my tote with the practiced subtlety of a woman who has, on occasion, jotted damning details in the margins of church bulletins. With a deliberate flick of my pen, I scribbled.

Subject 8: *Blazer Boy (a.k.a. Twitchy)*

Distinguishing features: Receding hairline, overactive sweat glands, blazer in tropical heat = poor judgment or poor cover. Behavioral notes: seen whispering with Captain Monty, visibly

agitated, poor poker face. Known associations: None confirmed.
Suspicious behavior: Hy claims extreme agitation in boarding
terminal; now pressing Monty with visible tension. Working
theory: Possibly knew Bart. Maybe not socially.
Professionally?

I tilted the notebook ever so slightly, just enough to catch the glint of curiosity in Hy's periphery.

He sniffed, scratched the edge of his chin. "Do I get to know what you're scribbling in that thing?"

I smacked the cover shut with a snap so satisfying it might've been scored by John Williams.

"It's need-to-know," I retorted, slipping it back into my tote. "And right now, you're strictly want-to-know."

His eyebrows lifted. "That so?"

I kept walking. "Unless you can recite the Dewey Decimal system backward, Detective, I'm afraid your clearance is pending."

He muttered something about librarians being more dangerous than murderers, which I took as a compliment.

Truth be told, I wasn't entirely sure what I'd seen, only that whatever passed between Monty and the man with the blazer, it wasn't logistical. It was personal. Emotional. Urgent.

And in my experience, those were exactly the kinds of things that got people killed.

"We need to see that body," Hy grumbled. I agreed, but had no idea where to even begin.

Did they store the dead bodies next to the mint chocolate chip?

We passed the souvenir shop, which had all the charm

of a fever dream curated by someone with a sequin addiction and poor impulse control. A spinning rack of postcards clacked in the air-conditioning's sigh. One bore the phrase **"I'm on island time"** over an image of a drunken coconut. Another featured a woman in a red bikini holding a martini the size of her head.

"Think they sell ship maps next to the novelty magnets?" I muttered.

Hy didn't answer. He was staring down a nearby stairwell marked **CREW ONLY**, his brow furrowed so deep I could've stored my knitting needles in it.

"I don't suppose you have a plan for how we get to the body," I pressed, watching him work out angles like we were pulling a museum heist.

"I've got half a plan," he grunted. "And two-thirds of a bad idea."

"Well, that's twice as much as most men."

He smirked.

We kept walking, veering off the main drag into one of the quieter corridors that wrapped the lower dining deck. The chatter and clink of mimosa brunch dulled behind us, replaced by the faint thrum of the engines and the occasional groan of aging ship infrastructure trying to hold it together for one more cruise.

"Your husband?" he asked suddenly. Not abrupt. Not nosy. Just… curious in the quiet way men of a certain age get when they've noticed you're not wearing a ring but still act like you expect the world to behave properly.

"Gone ten years," I replied. I didn't flinch. I didn't sigh. It was just a fact now. The way Florida is always damp, or how peach Jell-O should never be allowed in a salad.

He nodded. A small thing, but weighted just right.

"My wife, Emma, too. Cancer."

"I'm so sorry."

He shrugged one shoulder. "What can you do? Life goes on."

We walked a few steps in silence. It wasn't awkward. It wasn't sentimental. It was the type of silence you share with someone who's had their heart cracked open and taped shut with stubbornness and routine.

I could feel the story he wasn't telling. Not because he needed to tell it — but because we both understood what silence like that meant.

We reached a service alcove. A metal cart leaned haphazardly near the staff door, half-loaded with linens that had seen better days and maybe worse nights.

That's when Hy cleared his throat and nodded toward it.

"You ever push one of those?" he asked, tilting his head at the cart.

"Not since my niece's bachelorette party at the Holiday Inn Express," I answered. "Let's just say the 'police' involved were wearing their summer uniform."

"That sounds promising."

"Sounds *experienced*."

He gave me that half-smirk of his — just a twitch of lip that hinted he hadn't entirely given up on the humor section of life's library.

"So, here's the play," he said. "I get in the bin. You push. We find the morgue, do a little sightseeing. Maybe I get a linen rash. What's life without risk?"

I folded my arms. "You'd better not get stuck. I'm not calling maintenance if your back goes out."

He shrugged. "Haven't lost a stakeout yet."

"Well," I said, reaching for the cart's handle, "there's a first time for everything. Let's just hope your obituary doesn't read 'smothered in soiled towels during amateur cruise espionage.'"

He climbed in, knees first, then shoulders. I heard a few muttered curses about cruise ship ergonomics. Then, I draped a towel over the top.

And we were off.

Two pensioners. One dead body. A stolen maid's cart. And just enough plausible deniability to keep us out of the brig.

Maybe.

CHAPTER SEVEN

You haven't lived until you've willingly climbed into a wheeled coffin that smells vaguely of bleached corn chips.

I'd wedged myself into the cruise ship laundry cart like a man volunteering for a low-budget magic trick — minus the applause and with the distinct possibility of being buried under terry cloth. The metal frame groaned under my not-inconsiderable weight as I ducked my head, knees bent, arms crossed over my chest like I was practicing for my own Viking funeral.

"Comfortable?" Eugenia's voice drifted over the edge like judgment wrapped in linen.

"I've been cozier inside police interrogation rooms," I muttered. "And those had metal chairs and 300-pound suspects named Bunny."

"Now hold still," she said, and I felt the thunk of something soft and mildly linen-scented land on my face. "Towels incoming."

Clean, fluffy, warm-from-the-dryer towels, bless her heart. If I had to play corpse reconnaissance, at least I wouldn't smell like one.

She added a few more layers, humming something vaguely patriotic, then gave the cart a practiced shove that jostled my spine in three places and sent us rolling down the corridor like we were late for pole position at Indianapolis. I tried not to grunt every time we hit a seam in the flooring. Pretty sure the cart didn't come with shock absorbers.

All was relatively smooth — until we rounded the corner past the open-air pickleball courts.

I heard them before I smelled them.

Shuffle-thump. Cheer. Thwack. Shout. The unmistakable soundtrack of activewear-clad seniors battling for ball-based supremacy in the merciless Caribbean sun.

"Hey!" someone called. "Laundry pickup!"

Before I could say a word, I felt the first *thud* land on my head.

Then another. And another.

A tidal wave of sweat-soaked towels came raining down — hot, wet, and determined to suffocate me in the scent of victory and expired deodorant. I gagged as one slapped across my face, damp and disturbingly personal.

"Eugenia," I croaked from beneath a pile of what could only be described as athletic despair, "this is what dying smells like, isn't it?"

Silence.

The cart shifted again.

She was still rolling.

Pretending not to hear me.

"If I drown in old man musk, I'm haunting your stateroom. Permanently," I hissed.

Still nothing. Just the rhythmic squeak of cart wheels and her faint whistle — something chirpy and suspiciously unconcerned.

I sighed. Or tried to. But the next towel jammed itself into my nostril like it had plans to burrow.

This was the plan, I reminded myself. Blend in. Stay low. Gather intel. Find the body.

But as I marinated in *eau de old man*, I couldn't help thinking. For a retired detective, I still had a knack for smelling trouble.

Too bad it smelled like pickleball.

If the stench of despair hadn't already lodged itself up my sinuses, the thing that landed on my chest just might've finished the job.

It was elastic. A stretchy band with... a pouch?

Uuuughhhh!

Definitely not a towel.

I gagged. Loudly.

Not ideal when you're trying to pass for part of the laundry.

"Excuse me," came a voice sharp enough to slice pineapple.

Through the terry cloth veil, I went still. Real still. The kind of still that once got me through a six-hour stakeout wedged between a vending machine and a rat trap.

Eugenia faked a sneeze so violently it nearly knocked a vase off a side table.

"Bless me," she chirped, pushing the cart faster.

"I *said*, excuse me! Where is your uniform?" the voice repeated. I heard the jangle of keys that indicated someone with authority.

Crap.

Eugenia paused. I braced for the unravel.

But she snapped to attention like she'd just saluted in heels.

"I apologize," she said, voice syrup-smooth. "There was... a bachelorette incident. Strawberry margarita. My uniform's in the main laundry being degarnished. I was just on my way to retrieve it."

A long silence. I could hear the woman breathing.

"But I just finished reading a fascinating book—*Work Clean*, by Dan Charnas. About *mise-en-place*. Kitchen systems that apply to every workplace. Did you know a single adjustment in workflow can increase task efficiency by twenty-seven percent? I thought bringing these dirty towels down to the laundry at the same time would be an excellent use of time. I plan on doing it with all my duties. I call it... the Photuris Flow." Eugenia paused to take a breath, but she wasn't done. "I could do a seminar for the other employees if you'd like."

Don't push it, Eugenia.

Another pause. My heartbeat thudded somewhere under the mesh of sweat and humiliation.

"Is that so?" said the woman intoned. "I wish I had a hundred more like you."

Eugenia beamed. "Let's hope you never need them."

The cart rolled forward again.

"She bought it," Eugenia whispered. "Can you believe it?"

"No," I hissed. "She may have bought the Photuris Flow, but, lady, I nearly bought the farm."

She just patted the towel mountain.

"Shhh. We're not out of the mop closet yet."

I was still blinking back the horror of whatever elastic contraption had introduced itself to my chest cavity when I felt a shift in the air. Subtle, but distinct. The temperature had dropped a few degrees, and the scent of chlorine had been replaced by something colder. Cleaner. Sharper.

The light dimmed, too. The kind of industrial fluorescent you only get in morgues or frozen pea warehouses.

Then I heard it.

BANG!

Eugenia shouldered through a set of heavy double doors like she was leading a SWAT team raid on a Costco freezer.

"Oh, good," I muttered, clutching my cheek as the cart jolted over the threshold. "There goes my jaw. Dr. Chuckles is gonna have to redo my root canal at this rate."

She hissed, "I think we're close. Cold Storage, maybe." Then she turned.

Too fast.

Way too fast.

The cart's balance shifted with the grace of a hippo on a trampoline. I felt the back wheels lift and the entire world tilt sideways.

"Eugenia—!" I barked, but it was too late.

CRASH.

"What in the name of St. Nicholas of Myra!"

That voice!

***

Turns out that laundry carts are not OSHA-approved for evasive maneuvers.

In my defense, the cart was mostly upright when I left it.

Hy, however, was sprawled across the tile floor like a freshly unearthed archaeological find, dusted in lint, partially cocooned in terry cloth, and glaring up at me as if this entire fiasco were somehow the fault of my superior steering.

And then, of course, there was Captain Monty — looming in the doorway of Cold Storage like the Ghost of Cruise Litigation Future.

"Mrs. Drye," he said, in the tone of a man who has stumbled upon both a health violation and a liability waiver at the same time.

I clasped my hands behind my back, shoulders back, chin up. The posture one adopts when one has absolutely no good explanation and must therefore bluff like a champion.

"Captain," I replied pleasantly. "What a... lovely facility you have here."

Hy groaned and attempted to sit up, shedding a waterfall of sweat-drenched pickleball paraphernalia. One particularly unfortunate towel slapped the tile with a tragic wet squelch.

Monty blinked. Once. Twice. A man recalibrating his entire understanding of his senior passengers in real time.

I have been lectured before. By principals. By managers. By one very unpleasant woman at the DMV who became irritated when I asked for a do-over on my driver's license signature. I was morally compelled. The original looked nothing like my legal name.

But I had never been lectured by a cruise ship captain in a refrigerated hallway with a retired detective climbing out of a laundry cart in the manner of a disgruntled jack-in-the-box.

Until today.

Cold Storage felt colder now that the door stood open behind Captain Monty. A thin ribbon of icy air drifted across the floor and curled around my ankles. The overhead lights hummed with a faint electrical buzz. The stainless-steel shelves reflected the fluorescent glow in sharp angles. Every surface had the sterile sheen of a place built for produce and sealed containers rather than the presence of two seniors in trouble.

Captain Monty stood before us with the posture of a man who had spent years commanding storms, staff, and vacationers who drank too much rum. His hands were clasped behind his back. His jaw had a fixed quality I had previously only seen in stone busts.

"Mrs. Drye," he began.

Ah. The tone. The precise tone of a man who wanted to shout but had been trained by corporate HR not to.

"Mr. Reynolds."

Hy coughed. The sound held a familiar edge of suppressed amusement.

"This area," Monty said, "is restricted. That means

passengers, and I cannot believe I have to say this, do not enter."

I nodded. "I understand completely. And I do apologize for the—"

PAIN.

White-hot, toe-crushing pain burst through my left foot. Hy had stomped on my toe.

I jerked my head toward him, ready to deliver a whisper sharp enough to re-shelve a disorderly encyclopedia set.

Hy's eyes were not on me.

He tilted his chin toward something over Monty's shoulder.

I followed the gesture only a fraction of an inch.

A narrow gray door marked **SECURITY—CREW ONLY** stood half hidden in the shadows beyond Monty. The recessed lighting in that part of the hallway left the frame in a muted pocket of dim light. The door eased open a hair.

A thin man slipped through.

Twitchy.

His movements were quick and tense. The dull glow of the corridor caught the sheen of sweat on his forehead. His too large blazer appeared even more rumpled in the cold lighting. He shut the door with careful hands that trembled slightly.

His gaze lifted.

It locked with mine.

He froze.

I froze.

Hy's posture shifted in that subtle way he had when

his brain snapped a puzzle piece into place.

Then Twitchy fled down the staff hall with a skittering urgency that echoed faintly on the polished floor.

I inhaled sharply.

Monty turned. "Did you say something?"

"No," Hy and I answered together.

Never a reassuring sign. That tone belonged to couples hiding surprises and people who had just witnessed a man leaving a security office he had no business exiting.

Monty released a long breath through his nose. The sound carried the weary weight of a man who had seen too many cruise ship mishaps and had no interest in adding ours to the log.

"Mrs. Drye. Mr. Reynolds."
He pressed his fingers to his temple. "We pride ourselves on offering a relaxing, luxurious, and safe experience aboard the *Photuris*."

Hy muttered, "Felt very serene under those towels."

I nudged him with my elbow.

Monty straightened his jacket and continued. "So, from this moment forward, I must insist you restrict yourselves to passenger-accessible areas only. That includes the decks, the buffet, the lounges, the pool, the casino."

"The morgue?" Hy offered.

"NO."

The sharpness of that response bounced off the steel shelving.

Monty drew a deep breath through his nose and adjusted his cap. His expression softened just enough to resemble hospitality rather than impending detention.

"In fact," he said, "I strongly encourage you both to embrace the relaxing aspects of our itinerary. Tonight, for example, is our gala formal evening."

The overhead lights brightened slightly as a refrigerated unit hummed to life. The sound underscored the quiet excitement sparking beneath my ribs. The thought of a formal evening carried the scents of perfume, polished wood, and tiny elaborate desserts. I could already picture soft lighting on the upper decks.

"Oh," I said. "I do enjoy a good formal."

Monty nodded, clearly taking comfort in a topic unrelated to rule breaking. "It is called The Starlit Siren Soirée. Very glamorous. Very elegant. The entire ship will be in attendance."

The entire ship.

Every passenger.

All drawn to one glittering event.

Entire decks left peacefully empty. Cabin hallways clear of foot traffic. Cabin hallways near Bart's door.

A warm, fizzy thrill unfurled in my chest.

I attempted to hide my smile. The attempt was a failure. But thankfully, the universe distracted the captain.

A young crewman hurried up with a clipboard and a pen. His expression carried the nervous urgency of someone who could not proceed with his entire shift until he acquired one specific signature. Monty took the clipboard with a clipped nod and scrawled his name.

As the pen squeaked faintly on the paper, Hy eyed me. "Don't."

"I'm not doing anything," I hissed.

"You're planning something."

"I plan nothing." I lifted my chin. "Ideas find me."

The captain cleared his throat as he returned his attention to us. The sound had a pleading quality.

"Please," he said. "Go enjoy yourselves tonight. Dress up. Dance. Socialize. Do anything… anything other than sneaking around crew areas."

"Oh, absolutely," I said. "No more sneaking."

"Or snooping," Monty added.

"Of course not."

"Or investigating."

"Wouldn't dream of it."

Hy blinked slowly. The expression conveyed deep familiarity with the futility of my assurances.

Monty gestured toward the main corridor. "Enjoy the Soirée. It's a masquerade, so be sure to wear a mask."

We stepped out of the refrigerated hall and into warmer air. The transition carried the faint scents of citrus floor cleaner and distant fried appetizers from a nearby deck. The cruise ship interior lighting shifted from clinical brightness to a softer, golden ambiance. The muted thrum of engines vibrated beneath the soles of my shoes.

Hy walked three steps and muttered, "You've got that look."

I pressed the sleeves of my cardigan into neat alignment.

"I do not have a look."

"You absolutely do. The *I accidentally solved the Lusitania* look."

"I am simply appreciating that formal nights create strategic opportunities."

Hy rubbed the bridge of his nose. "Eugenia."

"The whole ship, Hy." I lowered my voice. "The entire passenger population will be dressed up, distracted, and nowhere near the stateroom decks."

He closed his eyes. Opened them again with the resigned acceptance of a man who knew his next several hours were predetermined by my enthusiasm.

"We are investigating Bart's cabin, aren't we?"

I smiled. Bright. Innocent. Completely unpersuasive.

"Well. The captain did encourage us to enjoy ourselves."

Hy released a low groan. In our established partnership, that sound meant I accept my fate.

"Look at it this way. If somebody spots us, we'll be wearing masks. They'll never know it was us."

"That is, if you can book it in those Dr. Scholl's."

I frowned. "These are perfectly sensible shoes."

We turned toward the passenger stairwell. The glow of evening lights filtered up through the open atrium. Somewhere in the distance, a string quartet rehearsed. The soft hum of anticipation spread through the ship.

The Soirée awaited.

And behind Bart's locked cabin door, our next clue waited too.

CHAPTER EIGHT

My tuxedo and I had always maintained a tense working relationship, and on the *Photuris* it finally staged a coup. I dragged the jacket off its hanger, and it folded itself in a way that suggested retaliation.

"Do not start with me," I told it. "We both know how this ends. You go on my body and I try not to breathe for a few hours."

The jacket refused to cooperate. I pushed one arm in and the sleeve twisted. I tried again, and the lining bunched under my elbow. My muttering deepened. "You think you are clever. You are not clever. You are hostility disguised as *haute couture*."

The collar snapped against my throat when I yanked it the final inch. The bow tie sagged before I had even tied it. I saw my reflection in the cabin mirror. A man in a formal straitjacket stared back.

For a second, I reached for the instinct I had relied on for years. I almost called out for Emma to fix the collar the way she used to, gentle fingers, quick motions, a soft joke about how a tuxedo never won against a Reynolds. The ache in my chest arrived before the thought finished. She had been gone so long, yet the space she left still shaped the room. Gloria had stepped in after, smoothing ties and scolding me with patient hands.

Tonight, I had convinced myself I could handle it on my own. I told myself I was not helpless. I told myself I did not need anyone fussing over me. Standing there with a collar that strangled and cuffs that pinched, the cabin felt too quiet. Both my wife and my daughter seemed a million miles away, but for different reasons.

I straightened the tie with stubborn pride. "Fine. Be miserable," I told the tux. "You are coming with me whether you like it or not."

Then I walked out to face Eugenia, knowing full well the evening would only get worse from here.

I yanked open the cabin door with enough force to startle a lesser woman. Eugenia Drye was not a lesser woman. She stood at the threshold in an evening gown that belonged on a royal postage stamp. Her silver hair had been coaxed into soft waves. A black, feathered mask framed her eyes. She gave off the impression of someone who had never once wrinkled a hem in her entire life.

She looked me over. Her gaze traveled from my crooked bow tie to the half-tucked shirt to the tux jacket hanging off one shoulder in open defiance of gravity.

She arched an eyebrow. "Are you going as Dr. Jekyll and Mr. Hyde?"

I scowled. It was all I had left. My collar was strangling me. My arms felt pinched by the jacket seams. My shoulders had been beaten into surrender. Something in my expression must have given me away because the amusement melted from her face.

She removed her mask. The feathers dipped slightly as she held it at her side. Without a word she stepped into my cabin and closed the door behind us. Her hand went straight to my tie with that firm confidence only a few women ever carried. Emma had had it. Gloria picked it up after her. Eugenia had it too.

Must have been in the handbook.

"My Robert could not tie his own shoes most days," she said. "A bow tie had the power to level him."

She worked in steady motions that calmed the air around us. No fuss. No commentary. No pity. Just presence. I had forgotten how much that mattered.

"There," she said. She gave the knot a gentle tug and smoothed the lines of my collar. "The tux will obey you now."

I cleared my throat. "Good. I was about to throw it overboard. With me in it."

Her smile warmed. Not bright. Not showy. Just warm. "Then it is fortunate I arrived when I did."

The room settled. My shoulders eased. The *Photuris* engines hummed beneath my feet. For the first time all afternoon, I felt assembled again.

"Ready?" she asked.

"Not even close," I said. "But that never stopped me before."

She slipped her mask back on and opened the door with a sweep that belonged in a ballroom entrance.

And for reasons I did not care to examine, I followed.

The entrance to the grand ballroom had been designed to impress people who traveled with steamer trunks instead of carry-ons. Light spilled from chandeliers that held enough crystal to bankrupt a small town. A string quartet played on the far riser. It wasn't Cat Stevens, but it was catchy. I caught a whiff of something that made my nose twitch.

"Half the perfume the women in this room are wearing probably costs more than my first car."

Eugenia brightened. "Ah! That's *oud.*"

I shrugged. "Yeah, I suppose it smells good."

"*Oud,*" she corrected. "Not *good.* It's produced when certain agarwood trees become infected with a specific type of mold. The tree tries to defend itself by creating this incredibly dark, resinous substance deep in the heartwood. That resin is harvested—very carefully—then steam-distilled into oil. Pure *oud* can cost thousands of dollars an ounce. Some people call it 'liquid gold,' though technically the molecular structure—"

"Yeah." I blinked slowly. "I wear Aqua Velva."

Eugenia paused, tilted her head with a sympathetic sigh. "Yes, Hy. We're all painfully aware."

Guests drifted around us in gowns and tuxedoes and ornate masks. It all had the sheen of a party that wanted to convince you everything in the world was perfect.

I knew better.

A detective walked into any room with a list already in mind. I scanned the ballroom with that old instinct buzzing behind my ribs.

Twitchy lingered near the bar. He wore a blazer that looked newly pressed, but his posture gave him away.

His shoulders hunched. His eyes scanned the room in short nervous darts. He kept one hand on his pocket as if worried it might vanish. The dim lighting hit him in a way that exaggerated the shadows under his cheekbones.

And finally, I caught sight of Lady in White. Her gown swept the floor in a slow whisper. Her mask gleamed. Every movement she made had the precision of someone who trained for high-society appearances. Her fingers clenched her clutch with too much force for a woman attending a party. She carried tension under all that grace. The kind of tension that came from a failed marriage and the threat of a vanished alimony check.

Two suspects in one room. I had been on homicide cases that offered fewer. Then I caught sight of a third.

The Hawaiian Hulk stood near the seafood tower.

"Well, that's certainly ironic," Eugenia muttered. "Well, it *feels* ironic, anyway."

"What's that?"

She gestured. "A man *that* size standing next to shrimp."

The big man looked a little green around the gills. His shoulders had a tightness that made every muscle stand out.

He squared his shoulders again, looking like he was one bad mood away from ripping apart the ice sculpture.

"All I know is that guy needs a serious attitude adjustment."

Eugenia adjusted her mask. "He certainly projects… dominance."

"Yeah, well, it's not the first time I've seen him throw that kind of weight around," I said. "Back at the cruise terminal, he grabbed Bart's hand. Not a handshake. More like a warning. Bart tried to pull back, and the guy held on for a heartbeat too long. You could see it in Bart's face. That flash of fear people get when they know something isn't over."

Eugenia's brows rose. "Oh, my. So, he definitely had a beef with Bart."

I nodded. "And when Bart finally yanked loose? His ring smacked the gang rail so hard it echoed. Loud enough to make people look up."

I snapped my fingers. "*That's* who Bart is — I mean, *was*. I knew I recognized him! He was the CEO of Centurion Enterprises. His picture was in the paper at the golf clubhouse yesterday. He was under investigation by the SEC. Yeah, I'd remember that obnoxious pinkie ring anywhere."

Eugenia stared at me. "Wait… did you say *Centurion*?"

My brow furrowed. "Yeah. Why?"

"Maybe nothing." She pursed her lip and tapped her chin, deep in thought. "Maybe something. Just a legal file I may have… observed."

Which meant *snooped*. I was beginning to understand Eugenia-speak.

She waved away my sanctimonious scowl. "Oh, get over it. My son is a lawyer."

"Was it something to do with the SEC?"

"No. A civil case. Rosetta Bianchi," she said. "Estate versus Reginald Bart. Civil suit. Dismissed with prejudice."

A quiet weight settled in my gut. "Dismissed with prejudice means the plaintiff has no further claim.

Someone ended up with nothing."

"That is correct."

"Motive enough for murder," I said.

"You think they followed him onto the ship?"

"Hard to say unless we can see a passenger manifest. That is a tall order."

She tapped one gloved finger against her purse. "I may know a girl."

I studied her. "You want to offer anything else?"

"No," she said with a pleasant smile. "I plead the Fifth."

I drew a slow breath through my nose. The room buzzed around us with laughter and champagne flutes and chatter about nothing of consequence.

"Well," I said. "Let us focus on the suspects we do have. Hulk. Twitchy. And Lady Macbeth."

Eugenia blinked. A spark of surprise crossed her features. "Shakespeare from you?"

"I contain multitudes," I said.

She gave a single elegant nod. "Evidently."

The shrimp station glowed under a spotlight that did nothing to improve Hawaiian Hulk's complexion. A server walked by with a tray of bacon-wrapped scallops. He brought a hand to his mouth and swayed. Sweat beaded at his temples. I watched him pace two short steps, then return to his spot, then pace again. That's when I realized he wasn't angry.

He was scared.

"He has walked to and from the buffet four times in five minutes. Either he plans to challenge it to a duel or he is terrified of something."

She followed my gaze. Hawaiian Hulk checked his watch again as if waiting for a countdown to disaster. He scanned the crowd with quick, jerky movements. His knee bounced. He reached for the shrimp but stopped, hand trembling. Something was off. A man that size should not look hunted at a party full of retirees and dance music.

"He is going to bolt," I said.

"Then we follow," Eugenia answered.

He abandoned the buffet at last and lumbered toward the glass doors that led to the promenade and lifeboat deck. We slipped into the crowd behind him.

The doors opened onto warm night air. Stars flickered above the upper decks. Hawaiian Hulk booked it toward the quieter stretch near the lifeboats. His shoulders stiffened, his pace slowing.

"We stay on his heels," I said. "If he bolts, I want to be close enough to trip him."

Inside, I already felt a shift in the air. Whatever waited around that corner had its claws in him, and I was not about to let it vanish before I got a look at it.

***

Hy did not need to say a word. His posture sharpened, and that told me we were trailing Hawaiian Hulk whether the ship encouraged promenade strolls or not. The deck stretched ahead in a quiet ribbon of shadows and soft amber pools of light from the lantern-style sconces. The hum of the engines vibrated against the railing. Hawaiian Hulk disappeared around the bend, shoulders tight enough to signal trouble. I felt Hy ease into that old detective rhythm and I followed.

We paused before the next corner. The air beneath the lifeboats carried a different weight. Cooler. Still. The distant music from the ballroom faded until only the steady thrum of machinery filled the hush. Then a voice broke through the quiet.

"You cannot disappear now." Twitchy, Hy had called him. To me, he was Subject 8. His tone held that nervous tremor I had noticed on day one.

Okay. Twitchy it is.

"There are records. Transfers. This will blow up."

Another voice responded in a hush I could not fully catch. The cadence told me the speaker was under strain. Angry. Determined. The breeze stole the words before they reached us. I leaned in, listening as closely as I dared.

Twitchy again. "You promised. This is your problem too."

The answer drifted in a breath that carried frustration. A sound that did not belong to any innocent conversation.

"Maybe he's on the phone?" I whispered.

Hy hissed, "Phone conversation my foot."

There was no point standing in suspense. Hy shifted his stance, and I moved with him. Years of instinct crackled between us, even if we had only known each other for a short while.

We turned the corner in sync.

Twitchy stood alone under the dim glow of the sconces. The rail behind him reflected the starlight in wavering silver streaks. The Hawaiian Hulk had vanished without a trace. No second silhouette. No movement. Only Twitchy, shoulders drawn tight, fists curled, expression trapped between fear and irritation.

He attempted a greeting. "Evening." His voice cracked.

Hy offered him a stare that could file paperwork. "You talk to yourself often? Or do your conversationalists usually evaporate into thin air?"

Twitchy swallowed. "Just a phone call."

"Only one problem. Where's the phone—or your earpiece?" I asked.

A breeze swept the hem of my shawl across my arm. Something at the standing table to my right caught my attention. A single glass rested on its white linen surface. The faintest red smear clung to the rim. A glossy mark. A very distinctive shade.

Venetian Tempest.

Alicia Bart's shade.

I kept my expression neutral.

Twitchy rocked on his feet. "You two need to stop this. Now."

Hy stepped forward. "We will stop when the man who poisoned Bart can explain himself. Now, where is he?"

Twitchy's brow pinched. "Where is who?"

I tugged Hy's sleeve. He shrugged me off.

"The Great Wall of Human. Big guy. Hard to miss."

I tugged again. Hy shrugged harder.

But Twitchy's jaw tensed. His gaze darted toward the glass before he could stop himself.

The moment shifted. A fracture in the mask. A truth ready to crack open.

And I felt the next move forming.

I nudged Hy and pointed to the glass. "I don't think he was talking to a man."

Hy's gaze followed mine. His eyes widened at the familiar shade of red.

Twitchy's reaction arrived too fast for him to mask it. The breeze carried the scent of salt and something metallic that heightened the tension already knotting the air around us.

Hy stepped in before Twitchy could look away. The muscles in his shoulders drew tight. He waggled a gnarled finger at Twitchy. "I remember you from the terminal," he said. "You kept saying he's gonna find out." Hy's eyes narrowed. "I think you were having an affair with Alicia Bart and he had found out."

Twitchy's mouth fell open. His hands opened in frantic denial, but I wasn't going to allow him to get off that easily.

"You're probably the reason they were getting a divorce, weren't you? But you couldn't stand the idea that she was going to lose all that money."

"What, lady? Are you crazy?" Twitchy's voice cracked, which only made him sound guiltier.

Hy growled low in his throat. "Crazy as a fox. Don't think you can outwit an old detective like me, pal."

"Like us, you mean," I said, because accuracy mattered.

"Well, I would have said it, but technically you were never a detective…"

"I realize that, but we are investigating this thing togeth—"

"Will you two stick a cork in it?!"

The sudden sharpness in Twitchy's voice sparked something hot in Hy. He stepped in front of me with protective instinct so swift I felt the air shift.

"Hey, watch it, pal. Hands off the lady."

That was when I permitted myself a quiet smile. Small. Private. Entirely satisfying.

I stepped forward again and pointed at the forgotten glass. The red smear glinted under the sconce light. "We saw you sneaking out of ship security. What were you doing? Let me guess… erasing the video that showed you poisoning Bart's drink?"

Twitchy blinked hard. His throat bobbed.

"Captain would probably toss you in the brig," Hy began. His voice carried a rough edge shaped by years of dealing with men who acted too slick for their own good. "I'd just as soon chuck you overboard. Guys like you make me sick."

I placed a hand on Hy's arm before his temper could push him a step too far. "Rest assured, we're going to alert the proper authorities."

Twitchy closed his eyes for a beat. Then he let out a thin laugh, the bitter kind that had no humor in it at all.

"Lady, I AM the proper authorities."

He pulled something from inside his jacket. The metal caught the corridor light. A badge.

Hy's breath left him in a rough exhale.

And even I had to admit the moment carried a certain theatrical timing. I pulled my readers from my clutch, drew them on, and leaned in to read.

"Office of Inspector General. Inspector Edgar Langley."

"Most people call me Eddie," Inspector Langley admitted as he pulled his badge back toward himself.

The promenade shifted around us. The night air felt warmer now, heavier, filled with the quiet thrum of engines and consequence.

"Well, butter my buns and call me a Southern biscuit," I muttered.

CHAPTER NINE

Eugenia's biscuit comment was still echoing when Langley snapped his badge shut and shoved it back into his blazer like he regretted ever letting it breathe the same air we did.

"Okay, that's it," he said. "No more questions. No more commentary. No more... whatever this is."

"Interrogation," I said helpfully. "You're the one who wandered into it."

"I did NOT wander—" he cut himself off, pinching the bridge of his nose. "Look. We can't talk here. Too exposed."

"Afraid your girlfriend will show up?" I asked. "Or Alicia Bart? Or the Hawaiian Hulk?"

He shot me a look that could curdle steel.

"Five minutes. Somewhere private. Then we're done."

"Lead the way, Junior G-Man."

He stiffened. "Don't call me that."

"Then stop acting like a rookie," I suggested. "Deal?"

He didn't answer. He stomped off.

I followed, grinning.

Langley veered off the main deck and into a narrow crew-adjacent passageway where the carpeting got cheaper and the lighting dimmed to "haunted hospital." He headed straight for a recessed nook full of stacked lifejackets and an emergency muster chart.

"Inside," he barked.

"Inside *what*?" I asked. "This looks like the coat closet they kept me in when I first made detective."

"Inside," he repeated through clenched teeth.

He was rattled. Rookies always got loud when they were tense.

I stepped in. Barely room for one sarcastic old man, much less three people and an entire shipment of flotation devices. Langley tried to flatten himself against the wall. He still took up two-thirds of the free oxygen.

"You sure this isn't a trap?" I asked. "No secret brig hatch you're about to pull?"

"Hy," Eugenia murmured. "Be nice."

"No," Langley said. "Don't encourage him."

I crossed my arms and waited for him to get to the part where he would lie badly. Sure enough, his eyes started doing that nervous side-to-side sweep.

"Start talking," I said. "Why follow Reggie Bart?"

"That information is classified."

"Perfect," I said. "So, it's fraud."

He flinched.

I smiled. "Ah. Embezzlement? Asset hiding? Creative accounting?"

"You can't infer things like that!"

"Oh, I absolutely can," I said. "And you twitch every time I get close. You're like a human Magic 8 Ball."

"I'm *not* twitching."

"You twitched right there."

His hand slapped the wall. "Stop, stop, stop. I should never have flashed my badge. This is exactly why new inspectors aren't supposed to talk to civilians."

"Civilians?" I asked. "Son, I've interrogated murderers in bathrooms smaller than this. I've got ketchup packets with more confidence than you."

He wilted.

We were getting somewhere.

"Look," he said, voice low. "I was assigned to observe Bart, okay? Just observe. It was... my first case off the desk."

I chuckled. Couldn't help it.

"You guys don't laugh like this when we drag you down to HQ," he snapped.

"At HQ, you probably have chairs and windows," I said. "And bosses who don't let you follow dead men onto cruise ships."

"I wasn't supposed to—" He stopped. "I didn't say that."

"You did."

"No, I didn't!"

"You implied it," I said.

Eugenia nodded. "Very plainly."

Langley groaned. "This is a nightmare."

"Then wake up and tell us why you're really here," I said. "Because you sure didn't hop on this boat for the buffet."

Langley sputtered. "I—I never said—"

"You didn't have to," I said.

That did it. Langley wilted, shoulders slumping, the fight draining clean out of him.

"I received information," he murmured, voice low enough that I had to lean in to catch it. "Unverified. Sensitive. It pointed to activity involving Bart. Financial activity. A partner on this cruise. Someone helping him move assets offshore. Irregular transfers. Things that—"

He clamped his jaw, realizing he'd already spilled more than he meant to. He slapped a hand over his mouth.

"Things that WHAT?" I prodded.

"That I am NOT telling you."

Eugenia lifted one eyebrow. He caved instantly.

"That could lead to felony charges," he whispered. "Happy now? My entire case is sinking, and you two practically greased the deck."

"You think the partner killed Bart?" I asked.

He recoiled. "If you think I'm giving investigative theories to senior citizens—"

I lunged forward. "Call me that again."

Eugenia touched my arm. "Steady, Hy."

Langley pointed a trembling finger at both of us, his inexperience bubbling to the surface. "Listen carefully. If either of you interferes in my investigation again, I won't hesitate to file obstruction charges."

I smirked. "Son, you'd better bring handcuffs and a forklift."

He shoved past, red-eared and furious. I watched him storm down the corridor.

"Rookie," I muttered.

Hy was still vibrating like an overloaded washing machine as Langley disappeared down the dim crew corridor. His footsteps faded, swallowed by the hum of the ventilation. The cramped muster alcove felt even smaller without his anxious huffing fogging up the air.

"Well," I said, smoothing my shawl where it had wrinkled against the stack of lifejackets, "he handled that beautifully."

Hy snorted. A sound of pure disdain. "Kid practically gift-wrapped his entire case and handed it to us."

"Men tend to overshare when cornered by a woman. It's why cross-examination training comes in so handy."

Hy looked at me. "You've done cross-examination?"

"No," I said sweetly. "But my son has, and I think I soaked it up by osmosis."

The muster alcove pressed around us, a triangle of shadows, rubber, and emergency signage. The ship hummed beneath our feet — a steady mechanical heartbeat that reminded me the night was moving on, and the investigation with it, whether Langley wanted our help or not.

And he did need it. *Badly.*

I stayed exactly where I was, adjusting myself against a lifejacket shelf while Hy braced an elbow on the opposite wall. The alcove forced us close enough that Hy's breath ruffled the loose curls near my ear.

"Let us review," I said, slipping into the cadence I used on library interns who were about to misfile something crucial. "Alicia Bart went to the federal government claiming her husband was hiding assets."

Hy grunted. "Checks out. He had the look of a man who could build a boat out of paper and pretend it's a yacht."

"He was meeting a partner here. On this ship."

"Someone with enough motivation to kill him," Hy said. "Which gives us a pretty cozy suspect list."

"Indeed."

"And now the only federal agent on board is—"

"A bundle of anxiety wrapped in a blazer," I finished.

Hy laughed under his breath. "You're not wrong."

I shifted, bumping the emergency flashlight box. Brass pipes rattled overhead as the ship adjusted course. It was remarkable how far from glamorous a luxury cruise became once you stepped five feet out of the guest corridors.

"Langley is inexperienced," I said. "He will be easy to rattle. But that also means he is easy to read."

"Already proved that," Hy said. "He cracked open like a walnut."

I allowed myself a small nod. "Which means the bad guys will see him coming from a mile out. And which also means we now know," I ticked the data off on my fingers, "Alicia was the whistleblower. There is an accomplice involved. That accomplice is likely on board. And Bart's death makes the accomplice's exposure far more dangerous."

Hy grumbled. "Adds up to motive, method, opportunity."

"And panic." I gestured toward where Langley had stormed off. "Hawaiian Hulk looked worried tonight."

"Yeah," Hy said. "He looked like he was waiting for the Grim Reaper to tap him on the shoulder."

"Meaning he knows something. Or someone."

"And Langley's going to butterfingers all of it."

"But we won't."

The alcove reverberated faintly with the muffled pulse of ballroom music drifting through the metal bulkhead. I adjusted my mask as I considered the map of facts unfolding in my mind.

"Bart's partner," I said quietly, "is likely not who Langley suspects. Otherwise, he would not be this off-balance."

Hy rubbed his chin. "Or he suspects them but has no proof."

"Which," I replied, "is the same thing as not suspecting them at all."

He chuckled. "You really missed your calling."

"I did not," I said. "I adored being a librarian. It taught me every investigative tool I need. Sorting, cross-referencing, and knowing exactly where to look when someone lies about returning a book." I crossed my arms. "Mildred Jansen never fooled me once."

Hy barked out a laugh that echoed unpleasantly off the metal walls, making two lifejackets jiggle on their hooks.

But the humor faded as quickly as it came.

"Eugenia," he said more soberly, "this thing is getting bigger."

"I know."

"And the kid's right. We ARE interfering."

"I know that too."

"Does it bother you?"

"Hy," I said, "I am seventy-two years old. If they haven't arrested me for my opinions yet, they never will."

A swell of music thumped faintly from the ballroom overhead, and somewhere distant, a steward's cart squeaked past. The alcove no longer felt confining — only transitional. A pause before action.

Hy exhaled slow and steady. "So, what's our next move?"

I lifted my chin. "We watch. We listen. We follow the money. We observe our suspects. And we let Mr. Langley continue panicking himself into confession."

Hy grinned, that sly old-detective grin that said he'd already decided we were in this whether the federal government liked it or not.

"Eugenia Drye," he said, "you're dangerous."

"Thank you," I replied.

Finally, we stepped out of the muster alcove together — two seniors with no intention whatsoever of keeping our noses out of anything.

"So, who's Bart's partner, you think?" Hy asked.

"Personally, I prefer to get my gossip — my information — straight from the horse's mouth," I said. "Everyone's here at the soiree. What do you say we go exploring and rustle around in Mr. Bart's unmentionables?"

Hy side-eyed me. "If you mean poke around the dead man's cabin, I'm in. But if that's some sort of weird kink, we need to reevaluate this relationship."

CHAPTER TEN

We spilled out of the muster alcove as Langley's footsteps faded. I sucked in a breath like a man who'd been released from Tupperware. The corridor out here wasn't much bigger, but after being wedged between a wall of life jackets and a federal agent having a nervous breakdown, even the low ceiling felt luxurious.

The crew-access hallway stretched ahead—dimmer lights, cheaper carpet, a faint smell of bleach and diesel baked into the walls. *The Photuris* hid her pretty bits up front. Everything back here felt like the working guts of the ship.

Eugenia adjusted her shawl. "That was… illuminating."

"That was a migraine with feet," I corrected.

We set off down the service corridor, keeping our voices low. The hum of machinery pulsed through the decking, steady as a heartbeat. Crew voices echoed faintly from deeper behind the scenes—too far to worry about.

I shoved my hands in my pockets. "The kid said there's a partner on board. A financial accomplice."

Eugenia nodded. "And if Bart intended to flee with assets, someone else intended to stop him."

"And I intend," I grunted, "to find out which rat on this boat was chewing on his bank accounts."

All the answers we needed were likely sitting in Bart's cabin.

Which brought us to our next very illegal step.

The guest corridors were a whole different world once we climbed out of the crew wing — warm lighting, cushy carpet, and a faint vanilla scent that made me suspicious. Nothing on a cruise ship smelled that pleasant naturally.

According to Eugenia's notes — **Charge it to cabin 9274** — Bart's cabin was midship, starboard. Conveniently close to the fancy suites but not fancy enough to require staff hovering.

We did a pass down the hall first to check for foot traffic. A couple in matching sequins tottered by on their way to the formal night festivities. Another guest yawned his way into the elevator.

Then the corridor emptied.

I jerked my head toward Bart's door. *Time to commit a felony.*

We marched right up to cabin 9274.

I grabbed the handle. Damn. Locked. And I mean solid.

I muttered a word I didn't often repeat in polite company.

Eugenia, bless her, leaned in. "Perhaps we try the credit card trick. They did that all the time on *Magnum*

P.I."

I stared at her.

"You DO know these locks are RFID, right?"

She shrugged like I'd interrupted her knitting. "Tom Selleck made it look very smooth."

"He also wore five-inch shorts and solved crimes with a mustache."

"So, that's a no?"

"That's a hard no."

Then luck rolled our way in the form of a housekeeping cart squeaking down the corridor. The maid stopped at the cabin next door, 9276, smiled at us, and propped the door open while she bent out of sight to gather a stack of clean towels.

Eugenia looked at me.

I looked at her.

"We should not," I whispered.

"We absolutely should," she whispered back.

And we slipped inside before she could look up and spot us.

The neighboring cabin smelled faintly of B.O. and someone else's sunscreen.

Eugenia wrinkled her nose. "People are animals," she commented as she surveyed the empty pizza boxes and the overflowing waste can.

I grabbed her hand and pulled. "I'll write up a 374.4."

Eugenia raised one eyebrow. "Dewey Decimal or California Penal Code?"

"This place qualifies for both. Now, move your keister, or we're gonna be the ones that get written up."

The ocean wind blew through a cracked balcony door,

carrying the cool, briny scent of open sea. We slipped through it just as housekeeping came into the room.

One problem avoided. I turned to face the next.

The balcony divider was waist-high metal with a decorative lip — basically a gym obstacle designed by someone who hated knees.

"All right," I whispered, sucking in a breath. "I'll go over first—"

Before the words left my mouth, Eugenia bent me over, hitched up her dress, and put a foot on my shoulder.

"Please don't—"

Her second foot found my head.

"—do that."

She swung over like a librarian who moonlit as a trapeze artist, landing with a soft grunt on Bart's balcony.

I straightened and stationed my hands on my hips. "I'll be damned."

"Come on, you lollygagger," she hissed, waving me over.

I hauled myself up, got my foot stuck on the railing, and face-planted directly into the metal divider. My mask, which I had valiantly tried to keep intact, crunched under me.

"You crushed it," Eugenia said.

"Yes," I groaned. "I noticed."

Then I spotted something that made the pain worth it. Bart's balcony door wasn't locked. Eugenia pointed silently. Scuff marks near the latch.

It was cracked open.

Someone had been here. Recently.

"Stay sharp," I murmured. I pushed it open.

Bart's cabin had the faint, stale smell of expensive cologne and cigars.

So much for the ship's "no smoking" policy.

The bedside lamp glowed on low, giving the room a hollow, abandoned feel.

I checked the bathroom. Empty. Shower dry. A toothbrush lay on the counter as if he'd used it last night.

"Three minutes," I told Eugenia.

"Two," she countered.

I stepped into Bart's bathroom, doing the habitual sweep I'd done a thousand times as a detective — old instincts, creaky but still working. Didn't expect much. Figured Langley had already been through it if he had half a brain.

Then I saw it.

Sitting on the counter was a sleek little bottle identical to the one I'd emptied in my own cabin yesterday — the fancy "Ocean Mist Ultra-Hydrating Kelp Moisturizer" included in the complimentary toiletries.

I had been surprised at how good it was. Wasn't proud of it — all this newfangled "manscaping" business was for the birds. But admittedly, my elbows had never been softer.

"Well, hello there," I murmured before I could stop myself.

Eugenia immediately appeared at the door, sounding like a woman preparing to scold a toddler. "Hy," she warned.

"What? It's not evidence. It's lotion."

"Lotion that belongs to a dead man."

"Dead men don't moisturize, Eugenia."

She stared at me like I'd just announced I ate evidence for breakfast instead of oatmeal.

I pocketed it anyway.

She pinched the bridge of her nose and muttered something that sounded suspiciously like *criminal accessory via skincare theft,* but I pretended not to hear it.

Next stop? The safe. Its latch sat slightly ajar. I frowned. Lazy, careless, or interrupted? Inside sat a passport, a money belt stuffed tight, and a stack of documents.

"François Aubergine. Looks like Mr. Bart was trying on a new identity."

"And he went with eggplant? That's the problem with people today. No imagination. Although," she stuck a finger in the air, "there's a pretty creative meaning behind the eggplant emoji."

"I don't want to know."

"You're right," she agreed. "You probably don't."

I pulled my phone from my pocket and started snapping, moving the documents with a pen I grabbed from the desk. I looked again at the stocked money belt.

"Forget saving for a rainy day. Looks like Bart was prepping for the forty-day flood," I muttered and picked up the passport with the handkerchief from my pocket. "And this cruise ship was his ark."

Eugenia called softly from the desk. "Hy… you need to see this."

The desk was cluttered with those cheesy cruise-ship photo frames — glossy prints tucked into thick paper mats stamped with the *Photuris* logo in gold foil. Twenty bucks a pop, and worth about three. Bart must've bought every single one taken of him since embarkation. And he had a Bourbon Cherry Bomb in his hand in every shot.

"Who actually buys these things?" I muttered.

"Someone who is in love with the camera," Eugenia said.

I snorted. "Yeah. And with his own mug."

Bart *had* grinned like a game-show host in that newspaper photo—even while being accused of fraud. Man probably practiced smiling every time he passed a reflective surface.

I picked up one frame, then another. Then a third. Something nudged my instincts. The kind of nudge I'd learned not to ignore.

"But someone else is a little camera shy," I said.

"What do you mean?" Eugenia asked.

I tapped the corner of the photo. "Look here."

Then the next one. "And here."

And the next. "And here."

Eugenia leaned in. Her expression softened into suspicion. "Yes, that's Laila."

"So, what's she doing in every single picture?" I asked.

"It's her job to be everywhere," Eugenia said. "It would be stranger if she wasn't."

"Sure," I said, "but why does it look like she's *ducking* the camera?"

Eugenia shrugged lightly. "She's not ducking. She's just… leaving the spotlight to the guests."

Then I heard something in the hallway. A cart squeak. "Time's up."

We scrambled onto the balcony again. The wind

slapped my face and carried the faint, distant music of the formal night. I swung over the divider first this time—mostly so I wouldn't get stepped on again. Halfway over, Eugenia grabbed my belt to steady me. That didn't help.

I still toppled onto the divider like a sack of potatoes.

We tumbled into the neighboring cabin just as the maid returned. She hummed, swapped out towels, and rolled her cart to the next door.

Only when her footsteps faded did Eugenia and I slip out into the hall.

I tried to push the photos out of my head, but something had started gnawing at me.

Like a rat.

***

The hallway felt different now that we'd seen Bart's secrets firsthand—sharper somehow, as if every decorative sconce hid another clue. I pulled my shawl closer to warm the nerves prickling along my arms.

Hy exhaled a frustrated huff beside me. "I'm telling you, Laila in all those photos… that's not normal."

"No," I said. "But neither is a fake passport."

His jaw tightened. He was probably still thinking about the safe, the envelopes we barely skimmed, and the balcony door left ajar.

I was thinking about the face in those photographs.

Laila had looked… worried. Or watchful.

Either could be dangerous.

As we reached a quieter curve of the corridor, my

senses settled the way they always did when a puzzle was finally taking shape. The air smelled of warm carpet fibers and that ever-present vanilla diffuser the ship overused. Probably why I kept craving Keebler Vienna Fingers.

A distant clang drifted up from the galley — pots being stacked or dropped. My shoes made soft taps on the decking.

Hy rubbed his palm over his face. "This ship's one giant alibi blender."

"Which means our job," I replied, "is to keep the ingredients separate until we know what belongs where."

He grunted an agreement that meant he respected the logic even if he hated the metaphor.

And for the first time since stepping on board, I felt genuinely certain. *We were getting closer.*

We slowed at an intersecting corridor. A pair of passengers laughed their way toward the elevators, champagne flutes in hand. No one looked suspicious until you remembered that murderers liked to blend in.

Hy's brows stayed furrowed. "If Bart was planning to run, someone else didn't want him to."

As we neared the grander guest hallway again, the lighting shifted to a warm gold that softened every shadow. I straightened my mask, now slightly askew thanks to our balcony gymnastics.

"So, we have," Hy rattled off the evidence, "one fake passport, one money belt, documents which may or may not be incriminating, and a woman who appears in nearly every photo of the deceased."

"Don't forget one federal agent falling apart faster than my rotator cuff," Hy muttered.

"Which means," I said, "the burden of competence falls — regrettably — on us."

He grinned.

I couldn't help returning it.

We walked in step until the corridor forked — left toward Hy's staterooms, right toward mine. The lighting softened at the junction, a warm amber glow that should have felt inviting. Instead, it made the silence stretch.

Neither of us moved.

We both had the same instinct — keep going. Keep the chase alive. But exhaustion and propriety tugged us in opposite directions. I folded my hands, trying to appear composed. Hy checked his watch with the subtlety of a man trying *not* to check his watch.

"Well," he said at last, clearing his throat, "I should… ah… take my statins."

"Yes," I replied, nodding a little too quickly. "I should probably take my blood thinners. All those years of standing on my feet. Helps with the clots, you know."

"You know what I find helps?" Hy asked.

"What's that?"

"Compression socks."

I blinked. "Really?"

Hy nodded, dead serious. "Always keep a spare pair when I travel. You know. If you wanted to try them."

"I'll… uh… think about that."

He shifted his weight. I shifted mine. The hallway hummed under the ship's engines, a quiet reminder that tomorrow the mystery would still be waiting.

"Good night, Hy."

"Good night, Eugenia."

"See you tomorrow?" I asked, pretending it wasn't a question I already knew the answer to.

"Sure, Eugenia. See you tomorrow."

I turned first, my shawl brushing my arm as I took the right-hand passage. My steps were slow—not because of stiffness (though my knees certainly had opinions), but because my mind was still back in Bart's cabin, with the photos, with the eggplant passport… and with Hy.

Hy Reynolds was a storm system all his own. Gruff, irritable, sharp as a tack even when pretending otherwise. And despite myself, I had become accustomed to his presence—his gravelly commentary, his stubbornness, his unexpected gentleness beneath the snarl. It was surprising how quickly someone could become… reassuring.

But I pushed the thought aside and focused on the girl in the pictures.

Laila.

Sweet as sugar. Efficient to a fault. A cruise director who had checked on every table, every guest, every shuffleboard tournament with a genuine smile.

The idea of her being wrapped up in Bart's mess felt absurd.

Still… she *was* in every photo. Lingering. Hovering. Caught half-turned away, always just shy of a full face.

Not ducking the camera, I told myself. Just leaving the spotlight to the guests. That was her job. That was her nature.

Even so…

I tightened my shawl around my shoulders as I neared my cabin.

Tomorrow, I'd talk to her. First thing. A gentle conversation. A librarian's touch. No accusations—just truth coaxed into daylight.

Because if there was one thing I had learned tonight, it was this:

Everyone on this ship was hiding something.

Even the sweet ones.

CHAPTER ELEVEN

I woke up with my knees screaming, my back cracking like bubble wrap, and some yahoo three doors down slamming their cabin door as if auditioning for a demolition derby.

Standard cruise morning.

But underneath the grouch was the thing gnawing at me like a rat in a cereal box.

Laila. In every single photo.

Cruise director or not, that wasn't nothing.

I tried shrugging it off while I shaved.

I tried pushing it aside while I brushed my teeth. I tried forgetting about it while I reached up to brush my hair and decided the two strands weren't worth it.

But the detective brain wouldn't shut up. I grunted and pulled on my bowling shirt and ignored it.

Of course, in the hallway, I passed two housekeeping staff whispering.

" —tried to explain to her how impossible cherry juice is to get out of white fabric—"

" — oh, I know. Randy, the pool boy, said she was absolutely *hysterical* about it — "

A pause. Then, softer.

" — and to think that poor man was dead just hours later…"

My head snapped up.

Cherry juice. White fabric. Hysterical. Dead.

"Ah, hell. Can't ignore *that*," I grumbled.

Time to check out the pool and see what floated to the surface.

The glare off the water topside was brutal. My squint had a squint. A bunch of sun salutation people pretzeled themselves. I saw a couple of mimosa aficionados who would probably blow point-oh-eight. I looked at my watch.

"At seven a.m.? Thank God, none of 'em are driving this bus," I mumbled to myself.

And then there was him.

A harassed-looking pool attendant, wiping down loungers. His nametag read: **Randy.** He had the thousand-yard stare of someone who saw something and desperately wished he hadn't.

I recognized that look. Hell, I *invented* that look.

I jerked my chin at him. "Hey, kid. You look like somebody smacked you with a pool noodle."

He sagged. "Sir… you don't know the half of it."

"Try me."

He laughed hollowly, a corporate knee-jerk response if ever I heard one. "I'm fine, really. Can I get you a towel?"

I looked down at my bowling shirt, black slacks, and sensible loafers. "Yeah, no. This is my Sunday swimsuit."

We stood there, just staring at each other for a couple minutes. Sometimes if you let a perp stew in his own juices, he'd spill the whole shebang.

This wasn't one of those times.

"Okay, Stella, time to get your groove back," I muttered *sotto voce*. I cleared my throat and rolled my shoulders back. "This have anything to do with the dead guy and the argument you witnessed?"

His eyes popped like two Ess-a-Bagels. Best bagels in Midtown, if you asked me. He swallowed. Looked around. Lowered his voice.

"Okay, look," he said, rubbing the back of his neck. "Okay, so—yesterday? This lady and the dead dude? They were *fighting*. Like… really fighting. Hands flying, voices raised—full Telenovela energy."

"Arguing about what?"

He winced. "No clue. I wasn't eavesdropping!"

And the Pope ain't Catholic, kid.

"You sure about that?"

He shrugged. "Okay… *maybe* I heard her say something like 'I won't let you get away with this!'."

"And then what?" I asked.

He took a breath. "Well… okay, back up a second. Before all that, she ordered him a drink. A Bourbon Cherry Bomb. Extra cherries, extra syrup, extra everything."

My hair did that thing it always did when I dug up something juicy.

Well, at least it would have if I still had some.

"And, uh… right after she orders it," he continued, "she… kinda grabbed the drink off my tray."

I blinked. "Grabbed it?"

"Yeah. Like — snatched it. Said she'd give it to the gentleman herself."

"Bart."

He nodded miserably.

"Anyway," he said, "I go get the drink, come back, and that's when I walk straight into the argument."

"Then what?"

"She grabs the drink, and reaches into her tote bag, right? And somebody yells 'HEADS UP!'"

"Oh, boy."

"And this giant neon beach ball slams into me. Pure reflex — I whirl — and bam." He reenacted the moment with tragic flair. "I knock the drink right out of her hand."

I winced. "Let me guess."

"All. Over. Her. White. Sarong."

White. Alicia Bart's color of choice.

Randy the Pool Boy shuddered. "Looked like a crime scene." His hand flew to his mouth. "Oh, my god. I didn't mean. Oh, no. You don't think..."

"I try to leave the deep thoughts to the Nietzsches of the world."

"The whos?"

I shook my head. "Nevermind. And she lit you up, you say?"

"Sir... she *scorched* me. Full-volume meltdown. I thought she was gonna throw me in the pool. I've never seen someone so mad over a spilled drink."

My gaze sharpened subtly — not enough for the kid to notice, but enough to get the mental gears a-clackin'.

"Do you know who the woman was?"

Randy shook his head.

"Can you describe her?"

"Expensive. Even though all she had on was that bikini top and matching sarong, I could just... tell. Not a woman I could afford on my salary."

I chuckled briefly. *Try it on Social Security and a public pension, bub.*

"Thing is, I know I've seen that pattern somewhere," Randy continued.

"What pattern?"

"The one on her swimsuit and sarong. I just don't remember where. Sort of looked like fireworks, or sea urchins or something."

Sea urchins? What the hell was I supposed to do? Rummage through Alicia Bart's suitcases looking for a bikini with tiny, underwater mace on it?

I took a deep breath. Let's assume for half a minute that it *was* Alicia Bart who Randy had seen arguing with Bart.

There were two possible reads here: one, Alicia Bart had the worst fashion luck this side of a Tide commercial; or, if she *had* slipped something in that drink, it was never meant to hit the pool deck. It was meant to hit Bart.

And the kid knocking it over might've accidentally stopped something far worse.

I clapped him lightly on the shoulder. "You did good, kid. Thanks."

"This job sure isn't worth $1800 a month." He sighed and went back to wiping down lounge chairs.

As I walked away, I thought about the pattern Randy

had described. Was it unique enough for an identification?

Hell if I knew. What did I know about fabrics? I once bought dress socks labeled "compression" only to realize they were just tight.

But I knew someone who probably *would* understand a fancy floral sun-worshipping sarong pattern.

I headed to Eugenia's cabin.

Straightened my shirt. Not that it mattered. Brushed off my shoulders. Also pointless. Knocked once. Firm, authoritative. Knocked again. Friendlier. Maybe unnecessary.

No answer.

My frown deepened.

Where was she?

A kernel of worry started knotting in my gut. Hopefully, she hadn't gone off half-cocked and cornered someone alone.

"Crazy woman," I grumbled. "She's gonna get herself killed."

I didn't like starting the day without her. We made a damn good pair, even if I'd never say it out loud.

"Nothing like stacking a missing persons case on top of a homicide investigation." I wheeled on my heel and headed toward the buffet. If Eugenia was sniffing out a trail, I'd be willing to bet it would lead her to the breakfast buffet.

So, plan for the day: identify the mysterious woman, establish her motive, and locate one stubborn librarian before she ran circles around me.

***

I woke with a single mission shaping my thoughts.

Talk to Laila. Clear her name. Protect that sweet girl from suspicion.

Hy's detective brain was useful, but it could also be... pessimistic.

As the golden rays of the morning sun filtered through my balcony door, my eyes fluttered open. I stretched gracefully, and only mildly regretted the stiffness behind my knees.

I brushed my teeth. Rinsed the sink. Brushed my white hair. Pulled on my sundress. Wrangled my shawl.

I gave myself an appreciable once-over in the full-length mirror. I looked presentable enough to interrogate an archbishop, or at least a very polite young woman.

I headed for the Lido deck with the determination of a librarian about to alphabetize the entire Sue Grafton shelf.

Laila was setting out morning activity sheets, bright as sunlight and twice as warm.

She spotted me instantly.

"Ms. Drye! You're up early!"

"I try," I said, smiling. "And I was hoping to speak with you, my dear. If you have a minute."

"Of course!" She clasped her hands, delighted. "What can I do for you?"

I crafted my little white lie with precision.

"I was at the photo kiosk yesterday, you know, where they post all the fun pictures of everybody they take around here. I couldn't help but notice... you're in quite a few pictures with poor Mr. Bart."

Her eyes widened — not in fear, but in embarrassment.

"Oh! Goodness, yes. I'm always near the photographers. Cruise directors are the face of the ship." She giggled. "We hover, we smile, we make sure guests get their moment. I try to stay out of the frame, but sometimes, it's... unavoidable."

Exactly the explanation I had given Hy last night. Exactly.

She brightened suddenly.

"Oh! Here." She reached into her pocket and pressed two tickets into my hand. "Free entry to tonight's Mystery Night. For your 'little gray cells.' Like you said."

My heart warmed. "You remembered. How sweet are you?"

She shrugged modestly. "Even if she's not here anymore, my Nonna raised me right. You treat people the way you'd want to be treated."

Sweet. Thoughtful. Genuine. Nothing nefarious here. Or so I hoped.

"I offered some to that poor Mr. Langley, too. He looked so stressed. Thought a fun night might lift his spirits."

"What would the *Photuris* do without you, Laila?"

"Play nothing but endless bingo," she laughed. "I'll see you around, Mrs. Drye."

"It's Eugenia, please. You have a wonderful day."

I watched her leave, greeting passengers with a warm smile as she passed.

"What a ray of sunshine. Well," I murmured, "time to

the dark cloud."

I found Hy waiting near the coffee station, three cups in, pacing like an expectant father.

"Where have you been?" he groused, then waved his hands before I could answer. "You know what? Nevermind. You're here now, and you're okay."

I'm… okay?

"Why, Detective Reynolds. Were you… *worried* about me?"

"What?" He got a sour pickle face. "No. I just had something to tell you is all."

I smiled subtly. *Methinks the detective doth protest too much.*

He launched straight into the Randy the Pool Boy's story. The mysterious woman and her argument with Bart. Bourbon Cherry Bomb, the beach ball, the explosion of red across white.

Then he described the sarong pattern.

Poorly.

"Kid said something like it looked like a snowflake that lost a fight with a starfish," he said.

I blinked. "Hy… that sounds exactly like a silver sword rosette."

"A what?"

"Ah," I warmed. "A rare Hawaiian plant. They only grow in certain volcanic regions. A bit sacred, actually. There's a legend about—"

"How does this help us?"

I gave him a prim look. "Because that exact stylized rosette is sold in the ship's boutique. I tried to buy one the day we boarded, but the clerk said there was only one left. He hadn't had a chance to restock before we set sail. A small." I sighed, momentarily embarrassed. "I haven't been a small since Reagan."

Hy scratched his jaw. "Only one left, huh? You think the gift shop works the same way everything else does? People just charge stuff to their cabins?"

I could sense where he was going with this. "In fact, I think they do. You're thinking if we go to the gift shop, we could identify the anonymous woman and potential poisoner by finding out who bought the swim outfit."

"Bingo." He held out his arm. "Whaddya say, Mrs. Drye. You up for a little shopping?"

I grinned, looping my arm in his. "Certainly. And, just so you know, blue's my color."

We ventured to the retail promenade together.

I cleared my throat softly as we stepped into the boutique — all white lacquer shelves, glass cases, and overpriced sunscreen. A clerk in a crisp polo materialized instantly.

"Good morning!" he sang. "Welcome to Trés Photuris Boutique! Can I help you find anything?"

"Yes," I said brightly, stepping forward before Hy could open his mouth and ruin everything. "I was in here admiring that lovely sarong in the window. The one with the… ah… silvery rosette design?"

His smile dimmed. "Oh! Sadly, that one sold yesterday. The last one."

"Yes, yes," I said, placing a hand over my heart as if she'd informed me the Vatican had burned down. "Tragic. But if we're being honest, I need something for a more… full-figured gal." I looked down at my chest. "A bikini on me is like trying to fit two honeydews in a slingshot."

Hy coughed. It sounded remarkably like a warning.

But I pressed on. "Anyway, I just adored the pattern. Could you tell me, do you have anything similar? Something that could rein in… the girls?"

"Oh! We have just the thing," the clerk assured me, stepping toward a display rack with commission-driven enthusiasm.

Perfect.

I leaned in, widening my eyes with practiced librarian curiosity.

"And what about SPF ratings? I read an article once that beach wraps can actually provide sun protection depending on the weave."

He brightened, delighted to have a question he could answer with authority. "Some of them do! Not this one specifically," he grimaced at the one in his hand, then pivoted. "But it's still great coverage. And it's machine washable on delicate."

"Machine washable?" I echoed. "On a ship?"

"Oh, yes! Or hand-wash in cold water if you're worried. The dye is very stable, though."

Behind the clerk, Hy inched closer to the counter. He scanned the surroundings, tugged at his shirt collar, and eased behind the register while the clerk continued explaining laundering cycles with religious zeal.

"And the sarong? Could it be worn as a scarf?" I continued. "Or a shawl? Or — heaven forbid — a makeshift sling? I once tripped in Kilkenny and had to improvise after spraining my wrist."

The clerk blinked. "A... sling?"

"Oh yes," I said solemnly. "Very handy."

Hy chose that moment to lift the little hinged counter-gate behind her and slide himself in, creaking metal and all. It sounded like a ship anchor being hauled onto deck. I winced.

The clerk didn't notice. He was too busy demonstrating how one might theoretically knot the sarong over a shoulder.

Hy reached the computer. And then he began typing. I tilted my head.

Okay. Not typing so much as... interrogating each key individually before gently tapping it.

Tap.

Pause.

Tap... tap.

Stab.

He squinted at the screen like it was written in Mandarin.

"So," I rushed out, a little too loudly, "what sizes does this one come in?"

"What size do you need exactly?" the clerk asked. "It was the only size we had left."

"Mature," I quipped, fighting the urge to glare over my shoulder. Behind her, Hy hovered over the keyboard like a sophomore on a first date.

Tap. Tap-tap. Long pause. He mouthed each letter as he pecked it out.

I felt every excruciating second ticking by.

"I don't know that 'mature' is an actual size," the clerk suggested. "But I'd say you could be about a size 12.

Does that sound right? 8... 10... and here we go!" He held a glaringly pink monstrosity before me. "Let's go ring it up for you, shall we?"

Hy waved at me frantically, shaking his head.

I grabbed the clerk's arm. "And do you have a loyalty program?"

The clerk blinked. "A what?"

"A loyalty program. For frequent boutique... enjoyers."

Hy shot me a panicked look as if to say *Keep her busy!* I widened my smile to near-unhinged levels.

The clerk, bless him, switched gears. "Well, we do have a points system for onboard purchases—"

Tap. Tap-tap. Stab.

Hy's eyes lit up. He found something.

I talked faster.

"And are there upcoming sales? Hypothetically? Want to take advantage of that tax-free, you know!"

"Not that I know of," he said, trying politely to inch away.

Hy leaned closer to the screen, lips moving as he read. He gave a tiny, triumphant grunt that sounded like a walrus clearing its throat.

The clerk startled. "Did you hear something?"

"Oh! Yes!" I said cheerfully. "Probably my stomach. I skipped breakfast. My metabolism is just a dreadful little tyrant. I should probably go eat. I'll, uh, come back later for the suit."

Hy froze, his hands mid-air, trying to become invisible.

"Are you sure?" the clerk said, clearly uncertain, "It

will only take me two seconds to ring this up."

"Yes, *darling*," Hy oozed as he sidled up to me. "You really *should* get it. It brings out your eyes."

I leaned toward him and grumbled. "It's going to make me look like a piece of Double Bubble with feet."

"All for a good cause," he whispered back.

I scowled, snatched the set from the clerk's hands and headed for the cash wrap. "Fine, but you're paying for it."

"Worth every penny," he chuckled deeply and honestly. If I was being truthful, it was lovely sound.

Almost worth the prospect of looking like a wad of human bubblegum.

The clerk's fingers moved swiftly over the keys. "Perfect! Now, if you'll just tell me what cabin number?"

"9546," Hy offered.

I sucked in a breath. A tiny, stabbing pain lodged in my chest. My hand clutched.

"Eugenia!" Hy rushed to my side. "Are you okay? Do you need a pill or something?"

"No, no," I assured. "Maybe just a glass of water?"

"Absolutely!" the clerk replied and rushed away.

Hy sat me down on a nearby lounge. "Really, are you okay?"

I smiled weakly. "Your cabin number."

"What about it?"

"I just... wasn't expecting it."

His brow furrowed. "Why? What's so special about it?"

I raised my gaze to meet his worried one. "It's my... my husband's birthday."

A few moments of silence passed before he replied. "Oh."

The clerk returned with the water. I took several grateful sips and stood, handing it back to him.

"Thank you," I said, bowing my head to the clerk in gratitude she did not understand. "You've been *immensely* helpful. Let's go... *dear*."

And with that, I grabbed the bag with one hand, Hy with the other and made a hasty exit before the poor man could realize his point-of-sale system now had a new patron saint.

Saint Hy of the Hunt-and-Peck.

In the corridor, Hy folded his arms.

"So, Alicia Bart was our Lady in White."

I nodded slowly. "And she argued with her soon-to-be-ex-husband. Bought him a drink. Tried to hand it to him personally."

"And lost her mind when it spilled."

"Hy..." I said carefully, "we need to tell Langley. But it's gotta be casual. If we come at him hard, we might get escorted off the ship at the next port of call. We need to bring it up in a social setting, so he can't lose his cool."

A brilliant idea popped into my head. I pulled out the tickets Laila had given me.

"My little gray cells have an idea," I waggled the tickets in front of him

"Mystery Night?"

I smiled at him.

"Yeah, okay. Why the hell not? But no tuxes this time, right?"

We shared a look. Not romance. Not even partnership,

122

exactly. But certainty.

Two old dogs with the same bone.

And we headed off — straight into whatever the night had waiting for us.

CHAPTER TWELVE

I rapped on Eugenia's door with the kind of knock that ought to summon a prompt response. She was always early. The woman could probably alphabetize a tornado.

Instead, I heard her call through the door—bright as a bell.

"Just a minute, Hy. I am not quite assembled. Come in and wait."

The door beeped. I heard the mechanical deadbolt turn. I pushed the door open and stopped just over the threshold.

Her stateroom had the quiet hum of air conditioning and the faint scent of lavender sachets. Everything was arranged with a level of precision that made my spine straighten on reflex. Shoes in a neat row. Books stacked in perfect little towers. Her shawl draped so evenly over a chair that the crew should have photographed it for promotional material.

I shut the door behind me and muttered, "Well, would you look at that," under my breath.

"What's that?" she called out from behind the bathroom door.

"I was just thinking you could do wonders for our government."

What a cluster that circus was.

"A place for everything and everything in its place."

I grunted, pretending I was unmoved by her domestic symphony. Truth was, it hit me right in the solar plexus. There was comfort in order and the woman had more of it than the entire New York Public Library.

I sank onto the edge of her sofa and pulled out my phone. Might as well make myself useful. The photos I had snapped in Bart's cabin glowed on the screen. I zoomed in on the torn scrap.

...artnership...greement...turion...terprises...ali.

The stubble on my jaw prickled. I recognized Centurion Enterprises the moment the letters clicked. That damned article at the clubhouse had crowed about Bart for three paragraphs. And here it was again.

Well, half of it, anyway.

Eugenia stepped out of the bathroom, pearls settled against her throat, shawl smoothed and ready for presentation. I lifted the phone so she could see the image.

"Look. Take a gander at this."

She leaned in, eyes sharp behind those delicate frames. "I'd bet the last slice of fruitcake that's Centurion Enterprises," she murmured.

I nodded. "That's what I thought."

"That is the same company from Stewart's briefcase." Then her brows pulled together. "But what's that last part—Ali?"

"I was thinking some Middle Eastern surname," I said. "Ali is the Smith of the desert."

"Or," she replied, tapping her chin, "a first name."

We both went quiet for a stretch. Something heavy settled between us. More a recognition that the puzzle had gained a fresh corner piece.

But we did not yet know who the mysterious partner was.

One thing was certain, though. Langley had been right. Bart had not been working alone.

We headed down the corridor, Eugenia gliding along with her lavender cloud and perfect posture, while my knees carried on with their usual protest chorus. The ship had switched into its evening rhythm. You could hear it in the thump of distant music and in the excited chatter bouncing off the walls. Everyone else was ready for fun. I was ready for answers and possibly antacids.

"Look," I said, lowering my voice. "If Bart planned to skip town—maybe switch identities—the partner might have panicked."

Eugenia's pearls caught the overhead lights as she turned toward me. "And killed him?" she asked, all calm and poise, as if murder were one of the dessert selections.

"Or shut him up," I said. "Or stopped him. Whatever the reason, someone did not want Bart strolling off this ship with a new name and no forwarding address. I would bet a month of my pension the same someone emptied his safe."

We passed a wet towel abandoned in the hallway, proof that passengers' standards dipped after dinner. The air held the scent of sunscreen, citrus cleaner, and too many bodies who believed deodorant was optional after sunset. Eugenia paused to collect her thoughts, hands clasped neatly, while I tried not to step on anything that squished.

"Well," she said at last, her voice turning crisp, "then we are telling Langley tonight."

"Absolutely," I said. "Public place. Lots of witnesses. He cannot huff, puff, or stomp off."

We reached the mid-deck theater entrance. Blue lights framed the doorway, flickering in a way that suggested the electrician deserved a stern memo. Inside, the crowd buzzed with excitement for Mystery Night.

Good. Let the audience gather.

Langley would hear what we had to say, and he would hear it with manners.

The mid-deck theater looked as if someone had shaken a mystery-themed piñata until it gave up the ghost. Tables were covered with fake dossiers and laminated clue cards. Feather boas hung off the backs of chairs. Someone had scattered magnifying glasses everywhere, clearly unaware that fifty percent of the ship already traveled with their own. In the corner sat a cardboard safe with hand-painted letters that read "THE MYSTERY OF THE MISSING MILLIONAIRE." The lock was drawn on with Sharpie.

"Little on the nose, wouldn't you say?" I leaned over and whispered in Eugenia's ear.

Laila materialized the moment we stepped inside. Her smile could have powered the ship at half-throttle.

"Oh good. You made it," she sang out. Before I could invent an excuse that involved sudden gout or a catastrophic shoelace emergency, she swooped in and pinned a laminated nametag to my chest.

I looked down.

Detective Grumbleton.

"Perfect," I groused.

Eugenia received Lady Primrose. She accepted it with far more grace than the situation deserved, adjusting the tag so it sat perfectly straight.

Laila clapped her hands. "Now for our other cast members."

Alicia Bart stood near the buffet table, arms crossed so tightly her shoulders practically touched her ears.

"Alicia Bart, playing The Estranged Wife," Laila chirped.

Alicia raised a hand with all the enthusiasm of someone reporting for jury duty.

"And next," Laila called, "Makena Pali, playing The Business Associate."

Both Eugenia and I jerked hard enough to feel new muscles protest. My stomach gave a slow tightening, the uncomfortable sort that always meant trouble.

Pali, our Hawaiian Hulk, lumbered toward Laila, a little unsteady on his feet.

"Somebody hit the open bar early," I quipped. But then it hit me.

Makena Pali. Pali. Ali.

There it was. The name we had not been able to place. The missing syllable from that scrap in Bart's room.

"I'll be a monkey's uncle. What are the odds?" I muttered.

Eugenia whispered back, "Remind me to buy a scratch-off later."

Then Laila announced Langley's role. The poor man shuffled forward in a powdered barrister's wig that made him look both humiliated and slightly allergic to his own scalp. He was The Millionaire's Attorney and clearly regretting every career choice that had led him here.

Laila beamed at all of us as if she had single-handedly achieved world harmony.

I had a sinking feeling she had just gathered the entire suspect list into one brightly decorated room.

The moment Pali lumbered toward the prop table, towering over a stack of plastic handcuffs, I felt the prickling urge to grab Eugenia before an epiphany smacked her so hard she fainted into the feather boas. I hooked two fingers at her elbow and steered her behind a fake palm tree with fronds so dusty they gave my allergies ideas.

She blinked up at me in that patient librarian way that meant I had better deliver something worthwhile.

"Makena Pali," I whispered, leaning in so close I inhaled her lavender lotion. "Pali. Ali."

The syllables landed between us with the force of a falling anchor.

Eugenia's hand flew to her mouth. "Oh my heavens…"

"Yeah," I said. "That guy. That slab of volcanic muscle." Pali selected his prop folder with the gentle touch of a man evaluating watermelons for ripeness. "I don't think Bart was involved with some Middle Eastern sheik at all. I think Hawaiian Hulk is the partner Alicia Bart mentioned. And if he knew about that phony baloney passport... if he suspected Bart was about to rabbit and leave him holding the bag? Think about it. It all makes sense. The argument at the cruise terminal. The phone conversation I overheard at the breakfast buffet the day after Bart was killed." I did my best imitation, all big and gruff. "I'm not going down for this."

Eugenia nodded, although her eyes kept drifting toward Pali, who stood with arms folded across his chest in a way that made the entire room shrink.

"We have to tell Langley," she said. "Right now."

"Agreed," I murmured. "Before Mr. Protein Smoothie hears us talking."

She shot me a pointed look meant to discourage my commentary. It failed.

Some men walked into a room and blended. Pali walked into a room and the air checked its insurance policy. I needed Langley before this thing snapped shut around us.

And I needed him fast.

The improv mystery dinner was already underway, and it was pure bedlam. Half the passengers treated it as Shakespeare in the Park. The other half treated it as karaoke roulette. Every table had a faux dossier, a plastic magnifying glass, and a prop clue intended for people with more enthusiasm than sense.

Laila stood center stage with a fake pipe and a confidence that could tow a battleship. "Detective Grumbleton, you must interrogate the suspects," she chirped at me.

I muttered under my breath. "Interrogate them? I can barely stand next to them."

Before I could escape, a guest in a feather boa thrust her plastic clue card at me. "Detective, I saw the millionaire sneaking around the pantry at sunrise."

I stared at the card. "Congratulations."

She waited for something profound. I gave her a nod that suggested the profound part would be mailed later.

Eugenia floated past, perfectly in character as "Lady Primrose," offering alibis in a crisp British accent she definitely did not have over breakfast. "I can assure you, Detective, I spent the morning tending to my gardenias."

"Do you even have gardenias?" I whispered.

"Hush," she breathed. "Commit to your role."

"Somebody oughta have me committed for saying yes to this barrel of monkeys."

I straightened my nametag and tried to pretend it was a real badge. "I'll show these yahoos."

My coup of authority lasted all of three seconds before Laila clapped her hands again.

"And now, Attorney Lionel Locksworth will read the millionaire's final letter!"

Langley stepped forward, wig crooked, expression pained. He lifted a sheet of paper and began in a wooden monotone. "Dear... friends. If you are reading this, then my fortune has vanished and treachery is afoot."

A man in a glitter vest booed. Someone else yelled, "Project more!" Langley flinched.

Perfect moment.

I edged closer. "Langley. We need to talk."

Without looking up, he hissed through clenched teeth. "I am performing."

Eugenia slid beside me. "This is urgent, Mr. Langley."

He kept reading. "Only the keenest of minds will uncover the truth regarding my disappearance." His eye twitched behind the wig. "Not now," he mouthed silently.

"For the love of Christmas…" I grabbed the edge of his paper, crumpled it, and bellowed. "We know who killed Bart!"

That did it. He froze. The audience mistook it for dramatic flair and applauded.

Before he could respond, Eugenia's posture shifted. She inhaled sharply.

"Hy?" she whispered, gaze fixed beyond my shoulder. "They are watching."

I turned my head.

Laila stood nearby in her hosting stance, too still.

Alicia Bart held her script, unwatched pages slipping from her fingers.

Makena Pali towered over the buffet. His stare sharpened to a point.

They were all within arm's reach. A sudden shiver rattled through the ceiling. A loud pop. Then the lights dropped into absolute black.

***

A sharp pop snapped through the room. It mimicked the cue Laila used earlier to start the Mystery Night performance, yet this one carried a different texture. Less theatrical mischief. More rupture.

Then everything went black.

For a second, I waited for the usual theatrics. There should have been the clumsy gasp from the woman playing the heiress. The preloaded thunder track that sounded as if it had been recorded inside a metal trash can. The cheerful staff members who had burst in repeatedly with tiny clipboards and far too much enthusiasm.

None of it arrived.

The silence settled across the room with such weight it felt almost intentional. My instincts prickled. This was not the playful hush of staged suspense. This was the kind of stillness that belongs in forgotten wings of old museums at closing time when even the walls seem to hold their breath.

I reached for Hy's sleeve. My fingers brushed warm cotton. "This is not in the program."

His voice came back rough and close. "No kidding."

Something shifted near my left side. Not the restless fidgeting of passengers trying to orient themselves. Not the helpful bustle of staff. This movement slid through the dark with certainty. I sensed a body glide past my arm, close enough that the air stirred against my skin.

My heartbeat thudded once, hard, a sound so loud inside my chest I wondered if Hy heard it.

Someone was moving through that blackout with intention. Not curiosity. Not clumsiness.

Purpose.

And it was not the kind of purpose associated with a dinner theater mystery.

When the first spotlight flickered awake, it felt hesitant.

Then the rest of the deck snapped to life one bulb at a time, a painful strobe of confusion and startled gasps.

Guests shrieked. A man in a sequined vest dropped a plastic champagne flute that bounced twice and rolled beneath a table.

Hy sucked in a breath beside me. "Oh hell."

Because Eddie Langley was not dead.

He was very much alive, although dramatically wishing otherwise.

He sat slumped over the table centerpiece, clutching his side with one hand and waving the other in the air as if flagging down an ambulance from space.

"My pancreas," he croaked. "I have been stabbed in the pancreas."

Hy barked, "That is not where your pancreas is."

Eddie blinked at him with terrific offense. "How would you know? You were a cop."

"Exactly. I ate a lotta donuts. I know holes. And that one's nowhere near your pancreas."

The guests murmured in shock. A woman fanned herself with her Mystery Night script.

Someone whispered, "Is this part of the show?"

Another replied, "If it is, it is incredible."

Eddie sagged and whimpered, "I am a desk worker. I process forms. I audit invoices. My natural habitat has fluorescent lighting. I am not equipped for mortal injury."

Hy knelt beside him, muttering something deeply uncharitable under his breath. I pressed a napkin to the wound, and Eddie yelped as if I had stabbed him twice.

"Do not let me die here," he moaned. "I can't be buried at sea. I paid for a plot in Greenwood Cemetery... next to Leonard Bernstein!"

"You are not dying," I said firmly. "You have been stabbed, not smited."

His eyes fluttered. "Feels smited."

And around us the whole room buzzed, suspects everywhere, all three potential killers perfectly positioned for the act.

The night had become very real.

Hy leaned over Langley. "Hold still. You are bleeding."

Langley's eyes were enormous. "I am aware!" he wheezed. "Oh, God. I never even passed the field fitness test. This is a hostile environment hazard. I want it on record."

His voice cracked. It sounded faintly operatic.

I slipped around to his other side, gripping the back of his chair before he toppled. "Mr. Langley. Eddie. Please breathe. You are not dying. The wound is superficial."

He gasped. "It feels very... not superficial."

Hy shot me a look. "Superficial for someone who is not a Victorian heroine."

Langley whimpered.

The lights were up fully now. Laila rushed toward us, hands clasped beneath her chin. "That was not part of the program. Oh my goodness. I swear that blackout cue was supposed to be during Act Two. I really should alert the captain." Her eyes darted toward the doors.

Makena Pali stood a few feet away, enormous and unsteady, his face turning the exact gray of week-old oatmeal. The instant he spotted the blood on Langley's vest, his knees buckled and he lurched sideways. A passing ice bucket became his salvation and his victim. He emptied his stomach into it with a noise that made three guests flee for the railings.

I leaned to Hy and murmured, "Someone is unsettled."

He grunted. "Probably ate the shrimp."

That's when I noticed Alicia Bart standing two tables away, staring. At first, I thought she was trembling.

Then I saw it.

She wrenched her signature white handkerchief in anxious twists. She kept wringing it tighter and tighter, her gaze darting everywhere except toward Langley. Then, in her panic, the handkerchief slipped from her fingers and fluttered to the floor. She didn't notice. She bolted, nearly colliding with a waiter as she fled.

My breath hitched.

People do not run that fast unless their conscience has far more stamina than they do.

Hy grabbed my arm. "Where are you going?"

"What's that thing you old detectives always say? I'm following my gut?" With that, I darted after her, but she had already melted into the crowd which was quickly realizing this part of the evening was off-book.

I whirled around, looking for her in every direction, but she was nowhere to be seen.

"Cheese and crackers!" I stamped my foot.

Medics had hurried into the room and were attending Langley. Hy rushed to my side. "Where'd she go?"

"I don't know," I groaned.

"Well, I know one thing," Hy offered, a sudden serious expression overpowering his resting grumpy face.

"What's that?"

"Remember how I said we know who killed Bart?"

"Yes?"

Hy pointed to the floor behind me, right where Alicia had been standing. Her white handkerchief lay there, abandoned. I wondered if she'd even realized she'd left it. But the thought was superseded by another, ominous observation.

A jagged streak of red slashed across the corner.

My breath hitched.

Blood.

That was the first sharp, unavoidable thought. And it sent a cold trickle right down my spine.

Hy crossed his arms and sighed. "I'm going to go ahead and say we got it wrong."

CHAPTER THIRTEEN

Medical staff bustled around Eddie Langley, easing him onto the gurney while he carried on like they were prepping him for a Viking funeral instead of a quick patch-up. He had one hand clamped to his side and the other fluttering uselessly in the air, punctuating every groan.

"Ow! Gentle, please! This cruise line had better carry platinum-tier malpractice insurance. I refuse to be patched up by amateurs!"

He sounded so offended by the entire experience I half-expected him to file grievance paperwork from the gurney.

I stepped closer, mostly because if anyone was going to wrangle answers out of him before he disappeared behind med-bay doors, it'd be me.

That's when his hand shot out.

For a man insisting he was dying, he grabbed my bowling shirt with enough force to haul me forward a good inch. The kid had a grip—panic'll do that.

He dragged me close enough that his breath fogged my glasses.

In a strained, dramatic whisper — one he probably thought sounded like a seasoned operative instead of a scared desk jockey — he said:

"Find who did this. Nail 'em to the wall and I will forget all about filing obstruction charges."

I stared at him.

Obstruction charges. Right. Because *I* was the problem tonight.

I grunted. "You want to maybe not threaten me while leaking on the upholstery?"

His eyes bulged with earnest desperation. "I'm serious, Reynolds. Whoever did this — don't let them walk."

There it was. The real fear under all the theatrics.

I sighed, rough and resigned. "Don't worry, kid. We'll get to the bottom of it."

He sagged back, whispering something about needing a hazard stipend as the med team wheeled him out, still narrating his suffering like someone had a camera rolling.

Truce struck. Mess made. And now it was on me to fix it.

I'd barely finished watching Eddie get rolled off like a melodramatic burrito when the doors slammed open hard enough to rattle the fake candelabras.

Captain Monty stormed in with the stiff-backed fury of a man whose blood pressure chart looked like a NASDAQ ticker having a nervous breakdown.

Uniform immaculate. Cap polished. Expression one

flicker away from spontaneous combustion.

If you'd told me he pressed that uniform with the heat of his rage alone, I'd have believed you.

His gaze swept the wreckage — overturned chairs, dropped props, shaken passengers, Laila vibrating like a Chihuahua in boat shoes — and finally landed right on me and Eugenia. He looked at us like we'd just screamed "Iceberg!"

The man actually sputtered.

"My ship," he choked out, hands flailing toward the chaos like he was presenting a crime scene to God. "My *beautiful Photuris* is two incidents away from being rebranded as *The Death Boat,* and you two seem magnetized to every single crisis on board."

I opened my mouth to defend myself — something simple, reasonable, gentlemanly — like *'We didn't stab the guy, Monty.'*

What came out was more like, "Now hold on — !"

Meanwhile, Eugenia tried to look innocent. And failed. Spectacularly.

She folded her hands at her waist, lifted her chin a fraction too high, and widened her eyes with the serene calm of a woman who had definitely just Googled "how to appear blameless." The effect was less *innocent dowager* and more *schoolteacher hiding fireworks behind her back.*

I could actually *see* the moment Monty's sanity packed a suitcase.

He jabbed a finger at us as if selecting culprits from a lineup. "If you keep sticking your noses into official matters," he thundered, turning a shade usually reserved for beets and outrage at telemarketers, "I will make certain you never set foot on another Lumina Voyages vessel again."

I bit back the urge to point out we'd gotten dragged into trouble by virtue of not wanting a man to bleed out in a communal dining area.

Instead, I raised both hands, palms out. "Captain, with all due respect—"

He cut me off with the sharpness of a man who'd just had one too many disasters in the same week.

"There is *no respect*," Monty snapped. "Not from you. Not tonight. Not since you set foot on *my* ship."

Beside me, Eugenia made a soft, affronted noise—part indignant teapot, part church whisper.

I didn't blame her. Monty was sweating panic and authority in equal measure.

He took one step closer to us, lowering his voice to a near-growl. "Consider this your final warning. One more crisis, one more disturbance, one more of you showing up where you don't belong—" His jaw clenched so tight I heard something click. "—and I will personally escort you off this ship at the next port."

I resisted the urge to ask if he planned to drag us by the ears.

He looked like he just might.

Laila rushed in the moment Monty paused for breath, trying to smooth the room the way she smoothed table linens—fast, bright, a little desperate.

"I am so sorry, Captain," she said, voice wobbling around the edges. "The blackout wasn't supposed to happen during Act One. One of the stagehands must have… misfired something."

Monty snapped toward her. "Misfired? Laila, this is a Lumina Voyages event. We are supposed to maintain *standards*. Guests expect precision. Clean execution. Not chaos."

That did it.

A flush crept up her neck. Her hands, which had been fluttering by her sides, stilled. She glanced down at her fingertips—quick, reflexive, almost the way someone checks for smudged mascara—then folded her hands behind her back so neatly it could have been part of the training manual.

Most people wouldn't have noticed.

But I was not most people.

Eugenia saw it too; her eyes sharpened just a fraction.

I didn't know what Laila was hiding—could've been nerves, could've been embarrassment, could've been a streak of stage paint from all the props lying around—but something about the timing put a pin in the moment. One of those tiny details you file away somewhere safe.

And keep very, very still until it's needed.

Security poured into the room in a black-polo tide, radios crackling, boots thudding, enough bodies to make it clear nobody was leaving until they said so. Guests shuffled back from the center of the chaos, all wide eyes and raised phones, the usual reaction when something real elbowed its way into their vacation.

I spotted the handkerchief first. White, neat, wrong. It peeked from under a sagging tablecloth as if it had tried to hide and given up halfway.

I bumped Eugenia with my elbow and jerked my chin toward it.

She started forward, all purpose and good intentions.

I caught her wrist and growled low, shaking my head. "Evidence."

The word froze her in place.

One of the security guards snapped his head our direction, sharp enough to tell he had heard me. He moved in fast, scooped the handkerchief up with gloved fingers, and sealed it in a plastic pouch. His jaw flexed, and he gave me a hard look, the kind that suggested he wanted to blame us for everything from the stabbing to the weather.

The overhead lights hit the cloth through the plastic. The red streak across the center gleamed, bright and raw. A few guests gasped. Someone near the bar lifted a phone and took a picture. Another person swore under their breath. Makena Pali folded sideways and went down in a heap, the big man hitting the floor before anyone could catch him.

I huffed, heat flickering in my chest.

"Damn it," I said, and the words felt too small for the mess spreading out in front of us.

I folded my arms across my chest, the universal signal for I am done playing cruise ship games. The security guards were still sweeping the room with their clipboards and suspicion, missing the one detail that mattered.

So, I pointed it out for them.

"You might also want to track down Alicia Bart," I said, loud enough for the whole mid-deck to hear. "She beat feet outta here faster than a raccoon in a Jellystone campground."

Every head within ten feet swung my way.

Captain Monty went rigid. His neck tightened so hard I could hear his collar protest. He stepped toward me with the kind of righteous indignation only cruise captains and kindergarten principals seemed to master.

"Alicia Bart is a grieving woman," he snapped. "Her husband was killed two days ago. Now she witnesses this? Of course she ran. She is devastated. I will speak to her myself. Do not harass her."

I met his stare. I did not blink. Then I turned my head toward Eugenia. She already had her eye on me.

We did not talk. We did not nod. We did not even twitch. We did not need to.

We were absolutely going to harass Alicia Bart.

Security shifted around us, sealing off more of the room. Captain Monty barked orders. Someone complained about refunds. Someone else asked if this counted as a scheduled activity. The whole place churned with confusion. But one thing cut through the noise as the handkerchief sat sealed in its evidence pouch, red streak bright as an alarm.

Someone who was in this room had Eddie Langley's blood all over their hands.

***

Security kept multiplying. I was fairly certain they had not arrived in such numbers, yet here they were, expanding in clumps across the mid-deck — kind of like tote bags at a librarian conference. One becomes eight before you know it. Half the passengers were pale and trembling. The other half were still asking when Act Two would begin and whether they should tip the performers.

The handkerchief Hy had spotted lay sealed in an evidence pouch now, the red smear glowing through the plastic with all the subtlety of a siren. The whispers around it rose and fell in one hushed word.

Blood.

I muttered a very genteel curse under my breath. If only I had seen which direction Alicia Bart sprinted off to during the blackout. One moment she had been clutching her shawl. The next she had evaporated. A vanishing act worthy of Houdini, if Houdini had favored expensive sandals and nerves strung tighter than violin wire.

Hy was arguing with a security officer who looked as though smiling was grounds for termination. No point interrupting two immovable objects.

That was when something brushed my ankles. A tiny current of cool air, threading through the chaos.

I turned.

The port-side door sat open by the smallest margin, just wide enough for a guilty conscience to slip through. Not ajar. Not careless. A precise exit.

And on the frame, caught against a tiny burr of metal, clung a familiar thread.

White. Fine. Soft.

Alicia's.

I glanced quickly around the room again to confirm what my instincts already knew. Makena Pali was woozy but upright. Laila stepped out of the ladies' room, drying her hands on her pants. I couldn't blame her. If I had a boss as uppity as Captain Monty, I'd have trouble holding my bladder in check, too.

Every suspect still present. Except one. Alicia Bart was definitely gone. Just like Hy had said.

And all she had left behind was the faintest thread and the distinct impression she did not intend to be found.

Unfortunately for her, I had *every* intention of finding her.

And I had just located her first breadcrumb.

Hy was still planted beside the evidence table, supplying a steady stream of unhelpful commentary to the nearest security officer. I caught fragments as I drifted away.

"You really call that a perimeter...?"
"That is not how you question witnesses..."
"Son, if you keep holding your radio like that, you will poke someone's eye out..."

Security ignored him with the rigid determination of people clinging to professionalism by their fingernails.

Which made slipping through the port-side door remarkably easy.

The latch clicked softly behind me, shutting out the bright panic of the mid-deck. In its place came a different world entirely. The corridor stretched ahead in two long, narrow arms. It smelled of recycled cold air and tired carpet cleaner, with the faint warmth of wiring humming a potent reminder that I was essentially strolling inside a floating machine. Cool air pooled along the floor, brushing my ankles again.

Left or right?

The left corridor pulsed with noise even before I

stepped toward it. The distant shriek of a half-sober bachelorette brigade ricocheted off the walls. Someone yelled "Shots o'clock" with gusto. A sudden chorus of the latest pop tune erupted with an utter disregard for pitch.

"Ever hear of autotune?" I quipped.

A second voice hollered back something about edible body glitter. I did not need to investigate further. It was the human equivalent of marching into a blender full of sequins.

The right corridor was the opposite. Dimmer. Narrower. The hum of machinery thrummed through the walls in a low and steady vibration. A soft, constant shush emerged from deeper in the ship. Water. Possibly the spa-level filtration system. I could see the carpet give way to tile in that direction.

I breathed in once and let the quiet settle.

"If I wanted to disappear," I murmured, "I certainly would not sprint into a pack of sequined hyenas."

I turned right without a second thought.

The lighting softened into a muted gold as I moved farther in, reflecting off brushed steel and pale tile. The air cooled, crisp and clean. My sandals clicked softly, each footfall swallowed quickly by the narrow passage. No voices. No footsteps. Only the faint mechanical heartbeat of the *Photuris* keeping time.

Somewhere ahead of me, a woman in expensive sandals and a state of emotional distress was trying very hard not to be found.

Fortunately for her, she had left just enough trail for a well-trained librarian to follow.

A few yards in, the air shifted.

Something warm and dark curled through the corridor, faint but unmistakable. I slowed, breathed in, and let the scent unfurl.

Oud.

Not the cheap imitation spritzed in department stores. This was deep and smoldering. It carried the warmth of burned wood left glowing under ash. A resinous sweetness threaded through it, the scent of an old cedar chest opened after years of silence. Beneath that lay a soft animal warmth, a sensual whisper that clung close to the skin.

I inhaled again to be certain.

Yes. Alicia Bart. I had stood beside her long enough during the safety drill to catalogue her perfume without meaning to. At the time, it struck me as a rather dramatic choice for a morning muster.

Now it served a far more helpful purpose.

The fragrance lingered in the corridor as if she had passed only moments ahead of me. It had weight and memory and a depth most people would have missed entirely.

My lips curved in a small, private smile.

"Well, now."

There it was. The little spark of pride I refused to name aloud. Hy would have tromped through this corridor with all the grace of a runaway plowhorse and never noticed a thing.

Who needs hunches when one has a well-trained brain?

I lifted my chin, pleased, and followed the invisible ribbon of scent deeper into the quiet maze of the ship.

Farther down the narrow corridor, something interrupted the smooth line of matte tile. A thin crescent of white rubber curved across the floor, delicate as a moon sliver. I stopped and tilted my head, letting the overhead light catch it.

A slim swipe of red lacquer marked the floor, the unmistakable calling card of a very expensive sandal. Clean. Sharp. Too new to have passed through a full housekeeping cycle.

Alicia's expensive sandals.

I crouched, knees protesting, and studied the mark with the same attention I once reserved for rare folios.

"She pivoted hard here. Someone turning fast, someone watching over her shoulder."

The words slipped out before I could stop them.

I straightened slowly, dusting my hands as a memory surfaced. A long, beige-spined volume from the reference section. *Trajectory-Based Interpretations for Crime Scene Technicians*. Dry as stale toast. Entirely devoid of romance. Certainly not *Fifty Shades*, which I regret to admit I skimmed purely for research into cultural commentary.

Still, the forensics text had been far more useful.

Well, except for that one scene…

I had a sudden urge to fan myself before I refocused. The angle of the mark revealed direction if one knew how to read it. A quick pivot. A decisive turn. A woman moving with purpose rather than panic.

The scuff pointed toward the Solarium.

I gathered my shawl, squared my shoulders, and followed the trail Alicia Bart had not meant to leave.

The humidity hit me the moment I stepped inside —
soft, warm, and clingy enough to flatten any attempt at
respectability my hair had left. It wrapped around me
like a damp shawl, carrying the scent of wet soil and
polished leaves. Behind me, the solarium door sighed
shut, and the noise of the ship thinned to nothing.

Fronds arched overhead, casting long, feathery
shadows that drifted across the tiled path like lazy
brushstrokes. Blue dome lights bathed everything in an
artificial twilight — an almost-too-perfect replica of the
moment before the sun gives up for the day. Even the
glass ceiling above had been tinted to mimic dusk.
Someone in décor clearly had ambitions.

A trio of fountains burbled in the center of the room,
each at a different height, their layered splashes echoing
quietly and giving the illusion of privacy. I knew better.
Spaces like this weren't for relaxation.

This was where secrets went to breathe.

I pushed my glasses up my nose. The humidity
immediately fogged them again. Of course it did.

Something flickered in my peripheral vision — a faint,
involuntary tremor that didn't belong to a fern. I angled
toward it, moving between the planters until a familiar
silhouette came into view.

Alicia Bart.

She sat hunched on a low chaise tucked behind a
massive Boston fern, her white shawl slipping from one
trembling shoulder. Her head bowed, dark hair hiding
most of her face. The polished, camera-ready woman
from earlier was gone; the person in front of me was
small, shaken, and alone in a way that tugged at instincts

I'd spent decades refining.

I eased closer, slipping partially behind the fern. Years of library work had trained me well—people tend to forget a librarian is present until she chooses not to be. I parted the fronds with the same motion I used to check shelf stability. Precise, silent, practiced.

The loamy scent of damp greenery pressed in around me. My blouse clung unpleasantly to my back. A bead of moisture rolled down my temple, and I willed it not to betray me by falling.

Then Alicia's voice cracked through the hush.

Her whisper was barely more than breath.

"It had to be done. I had no choice."

I sucked in a breath.

My heartbeat sharpened, each thump cutting clean through the warm fog of the room. I felt the weight of that sentence settle into me—heavy, certain, impossible to file under anything except important.

I'd just heard the kind of line no investigator in their right mind ignored.

CHAPTER FOURTEEN

I'd lost sight of her.

One minute she was next to me, muttering that the security guard's badge was crooked and that disorder was "how civilizations fall," and the next—poof. Gone. Slipped right out of the mid-deck theater during the swirl of security forms and medical theatrics. Eugenia Drye had an uncanny ability to vanish in a crowd without even wearing sensible camouflage, which worried me more than I cared to admit.

I scanned the room again. Nothing. No gray cardigan, no librarian bun, no shawl that looked crocheted by someone's great-aunt Mildred. Just chaos, irritated passengers, and Makena Pali looming over a terrified security guard.

Pali was large enough to blot out a small constellation. He had one ham-sized fist braced on the table and the guard pinned with a stare so intense it could have curdled cream. I couldn't hear all the words, but I caught enough: "rights… complaint… harassment…

jurisdiction..."

The second the guard started fumbling for a radio, Pali's expression twitched. Not guilt—fear. Genuine, gut-deep fear.

Then he bolted.

Not walked. Not briskly exited. *Bolted.*

My gut hummed. A man his size didn't run unless something serious was chewing at his heels.

Eugenia was missing. Which meant I had two problems.

And as usual, I had to solve them in the wrong damn order.

I muttered a few choice words under my breath, squared my shoulders, and followed the human Everest out the door.

Pali moved faster than any man built like a defensive tackle had the right to. He barreled down the corridor, shouldering past a pair of passengers and sending one gentleman's souvenir margarita splashing across the wall. I kept well back, letting the man's own panic set the pace.

He wasn't looking over his shoulder. Rookie mistake. Anyone running from something should at least show some interest in whether they were being followed.

He reached the stateroom deck—Bart's deck—and fumbled for a keycard with hands that shook hard enough to rattle the lanyard beads. The door beeped open. He slipped inside.

I didn't think. I lunged.

Got right up behind him and wedged myself through the narrowing gap before the door thunked shut. He never even noticed. The big man was halfway across the room, shoving into the bathroom, and the retching started almost the second the door slammed.

The sound echoed through the cabin. Deep, violent, full-body misery.

I grimaced. Sympathy had nothing to do with it. My own stomach pitched.

I had minutes — maybe less — before he finished reenacting *The Exorcist* in there and came out.

Time to work.

I scanned the room. Clothes tossed everywhere — wrinkled shirts, swim trunks, a pair of flip-flops that clearly hadn't been washed since 2014. The suitcase lay unzipped, its contents strewn across the bed.

And there, under a stack of resort brochures, was a stack of crisp cash with a ten-grand band.

My pulse kicked like a mule because I'd seen that exact pattern of banding two days ago in Bart's cabin.

"And apparently, it had friends," I muttered.

I stepped closer, careful not to disturb anything I didn't need to. The wad wasn't alone. Beneath it sat a crumpled document, torn at the corner. A corner I recognized. It matched the scrap we'd found earlier — the piece referencing Centurion Enterprises.

Son of a...

Makena Pali wasn't just in the soup. He'd brought his own seasoning.

Another retching heave arrived from the bathroom, followed by a splash that made my kidneys try to crawl north. I needed to hurry.

I peeled the document open. This wasn't some cruise

activity waiver. This was a partnership contract. A serious financial stake. Makena Pali wasn't just a friend of Bart's.

He was a vested partner.

And the kind of partner who might toss a cabin if he was scared something valuable was missing.

I checked the cash next. Ten-grand bricks, banded and neat, lined the bed like they were waiting for roll call. Ten across. Ten deep. Around a cool million by my count. Enough to ghost out of the next port and never look back.

The toilet flushed.

My entire spine locked.

I dropped the papers, lunged for the only cover available, and slid into the closet just as the bathroom door clicked. I grabbed at the hanging clothes to pull them around me — Hawaiian shirts brushed my face, their lurid colors glowing faintly through the louvered slats.

Pali staggered out, pale, sweating, moving like a man whose intestines had declared mutiny. He collapsed onto the bed, breathing hard. Then he picked up a stack of bills.

And started counting.

I held perfectly still.

Pali thumbed through the money slowly, lips moving like he was running mental math. Then he grabbed his phone, tapped a contact, and waited. He belched. Obviously, the flavor didn't suit him. He grimaced.

Someone must have picked up, because his expression changed.

"Yeah. I took care of it," he muttered.

My eyebrows shot toward my hairline.

"I said I took care of it. I'll get off at the next port." A pause. "No. I couldn't find it, but there's too much heat. I'm done."

Every word scratched an itch behind my ribs. "It"? The missing evidence? The motive? The murder weapon?

He grunted, ended the call, then put the phone aside.

And started *undressing*.

I squeezed my eyes shut so fast my eyelashes tangled. Every Hawaiian shirt in the closet swayed as I tried to quietly get my bearings blind. Fabric brushed my cheeks, and I could feel the pattern of dancing parrots judging me.

He stepped out of his underwear. A soft thump hit the floor. He turned. Walked toward the closet.

I whispered the shortest prayer known to mankind.

The door yanked open.

A massive, swamp-butt-level pair of underwear smacked me full in the face.

I might've blacked out for a second.

The door slammed again as Pali closed the closet door and lumbered back toward the bathroom, muttering about needing a shower.

The shower hissed on.

I slipped out of the closet, trying not to gag from the memory of what had just assaulted my sinuses. My legs worked before my brain did, carrying me across the cabin and out the door with a speed I hadn't summoned since my academy days.

Once in the hall, I exhaled hard. I needed distance

from that cabin. And a gallon of bleach. Maybe two.

But I'd also just solved a significant piece of the puzzle.

Pali had the missing money from Bart's safe. Pali had the torn partnership document. Pali had tossed Bart's cabin. Pali planned to flee at the next port.
Pali had told someone he "took care of it."

He was dirty. Filthy. But was he a killer?

I had no damn clue.

I rubbed my face. Something smelled faintly terrible. Then I realized it was me.

If this case made me smell like unmentionables one more time, I was throwing myself overboard.

But first—I had to find Eugenia.

***

Alicia Bart had just confessed to me.

Okay—not exactly *to* me, but in my immediate vicinity. So, I was counting it.

I edged in a little closer, easing between two oversized planters to get a better position should she spill any more mind-blowing tidbits. I leaned forward—only an inch, maybe two—just enough to part a curtain of fern fronds with the back of my hand.

My sensible sandal found something that was not sensible. At least, not to a septuagenarian engaged in covert operations.

A soft ridge. Slight give. Plastic tubing.

I looked down just in time to register the thin irrigation line coiled across the floor.

Too late.

My toe caught. My knee buckled. My center of gravity went decidedly *off* center.

I tried to correct the lean, windmilling my arms in what I'm sure resembled a startled Canadian goose attempting Pilates. The fern I grabbed for support recoiled instead of helping, shedding a spray of damp fronds across my face.

Then gravity finished what the irrigation line had started.

I pitched forward, slid straight through the Boston ferns, and landed at Alicia Bart's feet with the undignified thump of a woman whose evening had sharply derailed. A few fronds remained hooked in my hair, splayed outward as if cheering my arrival.

Alicia startled, clutching her shawl.

I pushed myself upright, brushing soil from my cardigan.

So, yes. That was my entrance.

The solarium fountain burbling was the only sound that penetrated the shocked silence that followed. Alicia had leaped to her feet, probably firmly convinced the po-po were bearing down on her full force. I decided to use that to my advantage.

I hopped to my feet, brushing off some clingy fern fronds and crossed my arms over my chest. "Ahem."

Alicia's eyes widened. "Are you following me?"

"That's what you do with perps."

I puffed up a little, channeling Hy's gravitas, which was difficult given I currently looked like a woodland creature who had barely escaped a lawn mower.

One finely shaped brow arched high on Alicia's

forehead. "Perp? Who are you supposed to be? Columbo?"

"I prefer Thomas Magnum, if we're being honest." I tightened my shawl around my shoulders and said, with as much authority as a retired librarian could muster, "Either way, I have questions."

Alicia arched a perfectly threaded brow. "About?"

"All the shenanigans that took place tonight," I replied. Although, admittedly, "shenanigans" might have been a little mild for attempted murder.

Get it together, Eugenia!

"When the lights went out," I began, doing my best impression of Hy's interrogative growl, "where were you? And what were you doing?"

It came out more nasal than growly, but the sentiment stood.

Huh. I did sound a little like Columbo.

She blinked. "Excuse me?"

I forged ahead. "You had plenty of motive to want your husband dead. He was going to divorce you. And I have it on good authority if that happened, you weren't going to get diddly squat."

She shifted her weight, scowling. "That's my personal business."

I ignored her. "And when Eddie Langley didn't drop the case against Bart's company even after he died? Well, that gave you motive to want him dead, too."

Her mouth fell open. "What?"

I shrugged. "If the company went bankrupt, you'd still wind up without two nickels to rub together."

"Of course," I added triumphantly, "you'd at least

have the money you stole from Bart's stateroom."

It was not quite Hy's style, but good heavens, it was satisfying.

Alicia stared at me as though I'd accused her of clubbing baby seals. "I didn't burgle my husband's cabin! And I didn't hurt him. Or anyone."

I folded my arms. I'd practiced this stance in the mirror once and thought it looked moderately intimidating. It probably didn't, given that my cardigan had a small appliqué of daisies on the sleeve, but one must work with the tools available.

"But your handkerchief," I said, pouncing. "I saw the red streaks."

She blinked. "Red?"

"Yes."

"Blood?"

"Obviously."

She tilted her head. "What are you talking about?"

I opened my mouth to explain when she suddenly reached into her purse.

I tensed. My heart skittered. Hy had warned me about cornered suspects. This was how people got stabbed with manicure scissors in true crime reenactments.

I scanned for a weapon—a chair, a fountain statue, a potted plant—and my hand landed on the nearest object.

A pink plastic flamingo.

Not elegant. Not intimidating. But sturdy, with surprisingly good weight distribution.

I brandished it with intent.

"Don't come any closer," I declared, hearing my own voice wobble. "I was on the Northwest Regional

Librarians softball team. Most RBIs in a single game—twelve. And the only player in league history to knock out a left-field umpire. Accidentally, of course. But still. I can handle a flamingo like nobody's business."

Alicia froze. Then sighed. And pulled a lipstick out of her purse.

Not a weapon. *A lipstick.*

I lowered the flamingo very slowly, trying to maintain some semblance of dignity while holding a plastic bird aloft.

"That," I croaked, "is… Venetian Tempest."

Alicia gave a smug little nod, the kind reserved for women who knew both their shade and their power. "Of course it is. La Rue Royale's top seller. Seventy-five dollars a tube. Worth every penny."

She twisted the cap off with a flourish. The red and silver bracelet on her arm jingled. The lipstick color gleamed—dark, dramatic, and precisely the shade streaked across that handkerchief.

Not blood.

Lipstick.

My stomach sank.

Alicia smoothed a fingertip across the tube. "The real reason I buy La Rue Royale isn't the packaging—though look at this cylinder, it's practically jewelry. It's because the formula is unbeatable. One swipe stays for hours."

I scratched at my arm, which had started to inexplicably itch.

Alicia gasped softly. "Oh, honey, you need moisturizer. Dry skin ages a woman by light years."

I stopped scratching out of spite.

"Anyway," she continued, "not that I'm obligated to tell you a thing, before the blackout, I reapplied and blotted on my handkerchief. And I was nowhere near that man who was attacked tonight."

I regrouped, adjusting my cardigan with what I hoped looked like investigative poise. "You could have run," I said. "Slim thing like you could have covered that distance in a heartbeat."

"Run?" she repeated. "My dear, have you ever tried running in five-inch heels?"

I had not. My highest heels were two inches, and even those made me walk like a drunk heron.

Alicia continued, "When the lights went out, I froze like everyone else. I stayed put until the world stopped spinning. Then I left. Quickly and quietly. I've already had enough people staring at me on this cruise already."

Her explanation landed with disappointing logic. Infuriatingly tidy.

"And besides," she added, "if I'd wanted Langley dead, I wouldn't have done it in a room full of witnesses. There's a great big ocean out there." She leaned in menacingly. "People fall overboard all the time."

I hated how reasonable that sounded.

I slowly brought the flamingo up.

Alicia leaned back, the elevens between her brows relaxing. "I may not have liked my husband. But I didn't kill him. And I certainly didn't attack Inspector Langley."

I studied her face. Her posture. There was no tremor in her hands. No guilt-smudged edges.

I suddenly froze.

"Inspector Langley?"

She blinked. "Yes. The investigator."

"I never said he was an *inspector*," I replied.

A tiny beat. A little blink. Her shoulders tensed, just slightly.

"Oh," she said, attempting a breezy hand wave. "Didn't you, though?"

"No," I said. "I didn't."

Her gaze skipped away, then bounced back as if she realized dodging my eyes would be the worst possible choice. She exhaled sharply and threw both hands up.

"Fine," she said. "Fine. You got me. I was Inspector Langley's whistleblower."

A beat.

Well. That was not nothing.

"I was the one who told him Bart would be on this cruise," she continued. "That he'd be meeting his partner. Not that I knew who the partner was, mind you. If I did, I would have turned *that* name in too."

She folded her arms, defiant in a way that looked suspicious if you didn't listen carefully — and exasperated if you did.

"I figured if Langley and the OIG and the SEC could keep Bart distracted long enough, I could… reallocate a few personal funds. Move enough to live comfortably before the whole house of cards came tumbling down. It's amazing what you can do with a good Cayman Islands account."

She said it as if she were discussing couponing.

My mind clicked through possibilities, crossed off several, circled others.

Whistleblower? Yes.

Self-serving? Certainly.

Murderer?

Not so neatly boxed. But was fairly certain she wasn't our killer, or the one who'd gone after Eddie Langley.

I lowered the flamingo completely.

"Well," I said, forcing composure back into my bones, "thank you for your time."

"And thank you," she replied, "for the… exercise."

I pretended not to hear the sarcasm.

As I slipped back through the solarium's leafy shadows, one thought anchored itself firmly:

If Alicia Bart didn't do it…

Someone else aboard this ship had tried to kill Eddie Langley.

And they were still out there.

CHAPTER FIFTEEN

I had patched a lot of people in my day. Partners with split brows. Drunks who picked the wrong bar fight. One guy who managed to shoot himself in the foot with his own service weapon. I had never, until that night, treated a librarian for fern exposure.

Eugenia sat perched on the edge of the lower bunk in my cabin, sleeves rolled to her elbows, jaw tight. Angry red blotches marched up her arms and across one cheek. The rash had raised little bumps that made my own skin itch in sympathy. The overhead light gave everything a stale yellow cast that did neither of us any favors.

"Hold still," I told her.

"This is barbaric," she sniffed. "You are not even measuring."

"Calamine is not a precision instrument," I said. "It is pink glue in a bottle."

I dipped the cotton ball again and dabbed at a cluster of bumps on her forearm. She hissed when the cold hit. I tried not to smirk. Tried and failed.

"It was one fern," she muttered. "One. People brush past foliage all the time without erupting."

"Some plants hold grudges," I said. "Ferns. Poison oak. Half the women I dated before I knew better."

That got me a narrow stare.

I moved to her cheek. The skin there already had a faint shine from earlier lotion. The rash had crept up near her eye. I dabbed very carefully.

"Do not give me spots," she warned. "If you turn me into a peppermint candy, I will never forgive you."

"You want the itching gone or you want to look ready for prom photos," I asked. "You cannot have both."

She huffed and stared at the far wall where the ship's artwork tried and failed to distract from the faint smell of disinfectant and ocean air. The cabin vibrated with the deep thrum of engines. Somewhere above us, the last of the Mystery Night guests were probably still arguing about whether the stabbing had been part of the program.

"Poison oak once got me all over my backside," I said, partly to distract her while I hit another patch near her wrist. "Late night stakeout in the woods. Supervisor said the car would spook the dealer, so we waited outside. I leaned on the wrong shrub. Spent a week walking bow-legged. Thought I would chew my own skin off."

"That is not comforting," she said.

"Good," I answered. "Fear keeps you from hugging shrubbery again."

A corner of her mouth twitched. I counted that as a win and reached for a fresh cotton ball.

By the time I finished turning her into a patchwork

quilt, the worst of the redness had calmed. The bumps still looked angry, but at least she had stopped flinching every time the cotton came near.

She drew her arms back toward herself, examining the streaks with critical eyes. "Functional," she conceded. "Cosmetically tragic, but functional."

"You can add it to your cruise scrapbook," I said. "Photos of sunsets, souvenir programs, chemical warfare on your forearms."

She sniffed, then lifted her chin. "I did not trip into that fern without cause. I have information."

"Good," I said, sinking onto the chair by the tiny desk. "Because I do too. You first."

She folded her hands in her lap, careful not to smear the pink. "Alicia Bart did not kill Eddie Langley," she said. "Or her husband. Or burgle the cabin."

"That is a bold opening," I said. "You planning to back it up or just throw it in my face?"

"I followed her to the solarium," she went on. "She thought she was alone. She said it had to be done. She had no choice. Then she admitted she was the whistleblower who tipped off the Office of Inspector General about Bart and his partner. She told them he would be on this ship. She hoped they would occupy him long enough for her to move her own assets before the whole structure collapsed."

I watched her as she spoke. No wobble in her voice. No uncertainty. She believed every word.

"And the handkerchief?" I asked. "The red streaks?"

Eugenia frowned. "Lipstick. Venetian Tempest. La Rue Royale brand. Seventy-five dollars for a single tube."

"And to think I spent all those years putting away drug dealers and murderers. Should have been going after the cosmetics companies!"

Eugenia nodded her agreement. "Anyhoo, she produced it from her purse and demonstrated." She scratched her forearm absently and caught herself halfway through, tucking her hand under her leg instead. "The shade matched the marks on the cloth perfectly."

"So, she is selfish, opportunistic, and morally flexible," I said. "But not our knife in the blackout."

"Correct," she said.

I rubbed my jaw. Another possible killer shuffled sideways into the gray area. It annoyed me more than it should have.

"That was my evening," she finished. "What about yours?"

I leaned back until the chair protested. "Mine smelled worse," I said. "And involved underwear that should have been declared a biohazard."

Her brows lifted. "I am almost afraid to ask."

"You should be," I said. "Because Pali is about three steps past suspicious now."

Eugenia straightened so sharply the bunk squeaked. "Explain."

I scrubbed a hand over the back of my neck, wishing for a strong drink or a weaker stomach. "After he cornered that security guard, he bolted. Not walked. Bolted. And not in the direction normal people run when they need to vomit."

Her eyes narrowed. "So he *was* running from something."

"He sure as hell wasn't running to the shuffleboard court." I leaned forward, elbows on my knees. "I tailed him back to his stateroom. Managed to slip in behind him before he shut the door."

She made a soft sound of alarm. "Hy. That is reckless."

"That's police work."

"You are retired."

"Then it's nostalgia."

That earned me a stare that communicated disappointment, concern, and a faint desire to swat me with a hardcover.

"Anyway," I said, "the second I got inside, he rushed into the head and started retching. Violently. Could've peeled paint off the tiles. I didn't have much time before he finished redecorating his insides."

"Hy."

"Exactly. So I did a quick sweep." I held up a hand. "And by sweep, I mean the thing you do when you know you have maybe forty seconds before a large angry suspect emerges half-naked and confused."

"Please get to the part with the underwear quickly," she said, bracing herself.

"It's worse before it gets there." I pointed toward the bunk across from hers. "His bed looked like the Treasury Department sneezed. Cash. Everywhere. Bricks of it. Ten grand packs. At least a hundred of them."

Her breath hitched. She didn't gasp — librarians don't gasp — but she came close. "One million dollars."

"Give or take whatever he stuffed in his carry-on. Enough cash to buy a private exit strategy at our next port." I eyed her. "He's not interested in scenic snorkeling, that's for sure."

She folded her hands, fingers twitching once toward a rash that begged to be scratched. "Hy... what was he looking for in Bart's cabin. If he had the money, what more did he want."

"A document," I said. "I found the rest of it on his desk. The torn contract that matches our little scrap. Centurion Enterprises. His signature space. His cut."

Eugenia shut her eyes. "So, he *was* Bart's partner."

"Bingo."

"And if Bart planned to run," she murmured, "Pali loses everything."

"Exactly. And he told someone on the phone that he 'took care of it' but couldn't find what he needed. And that there's too much heat."

Her eyes snapped open. "Hy. He is going to run at the next port."

"That's what the cash mattress told me."

"And the underwear," she said faintly.

"Oh, that part." I grimaced. "You don't want that part."

"I do not," she said. "And yet I know I will hear it anyway."

"He opened the closet," I said. "While I was inside it. I had to hide behind a sea of Hawaiian shirts. He tossed in underwear. They hit me in the face. I'm still in recovery."

She blinked once. "Hy."

"I didn't inhale."

"Thank heaven for small mercies."

I sat back and let out a slow breath. "Point is, he's dangerous, he's panicked, and he's planning to leave us

170

in his wake as soon as we hit Nassau."

She pressed her hand against her tote, thoughtful. "Then Inspector Langley needs to know immediately."

"Exactly."

She shifted, winced as a welt tugged. "Hy… we cannot let him get off that ship."

"Then I better go give Langley his bedtime reading."

I stood, stretching my back until something popped. Eugenia rose too but slower, stiff from both the rash and the indignity of being used as a calamine canvas.

"Before you run off," she said, "we should—" Her forearm twitched violently, and she sucked in a breath through her teeth. "Hy. The itching is returning."

"Of course it is," I said. "That's the calamine wearing off. You're due for a second coat."

I reached for the bottle. Shook it. It sloshed once and then gave up the ghost.

"Empty," I said. "We've got nothing left but…" I rifled through the toiletries on the shelf, grabbed the small fancy bottle with the gold top. "This."

Eugenia gave it the side-eye. "The moisturizer you stole from Bart's cabin."

"Borrowed," I said. "He wasn't using it on account of being dead." I shook it. A faint rattle sounded. Not a slosh. A click. Dense and metallic.

We both paused.

"That's weird," I said.

Eugenia tilted her head. "It could be one of those little ball bearings they use to blend contents in high-end liquids."

"Like spray paint?"

"Precisely." She scratched again, caught herself, and sighed. "Give it to me, Hy. I need something before I claw my own arms off."

I closed my hand around it and pulled it back. "Nope. I stole this for me. Steal your own expensive skincare."

She stared. Hard. I stared back. Less convincingly.

"Hy."

"No."

"Hy."

I held strong for three full seconds before my shoulders slumped. I handed it over with the same energy of a toddler relinquishing a stolen cookie.

She accepted it with maddening grace — then promptly slipped it into her tote without even opening it.

"What was that," I asked.

"Delayed gratification," she said. "I will examine it later. After I acquire actual calamine."

"You're going to scratch yourself bald before then."

She ignored that. "Laila will have some."

I frowned. "Why Laila?"

"She is the event coordinator," she said. "She has an entire closet of emergency supplies for frightened passengers and minor mishaps."

I eyed her. "This is about the blackout."

"It is about the rash," she said, then after a beat, "and the blackout."

I sighed. "Fine. I'll hit the med bay and handle Langley. You go get your pink goo."

Eugenia adjusted her shawl, winced, adjusted again, then gave up entirely and lifted her chin.

"We divide and conquer," she said. "You take Pali's

info to Langley. I pursue Laila."

"Carefully," I warned.

"I will use my gentlest librarian voice."

"That's what I'm afraid of."

She gave a thin smile. "Hy, my arms may be aflame, but my mind is intact. I can manage one conversation."

I moved toward the door, palm against the smooth metal. "Just don't poke anything dangerous."

"Hy. Nothing about this cruise has been safe."

"Fair point."

I cracked the door open. Cool corridor air rolled in, sharper than the stale disinfectant inside.

"Meet back here afterward," I said.

"Agreed."

We stepped into the hall, the engines humming beneath us, the ship rolling steadily as a heartbeat. Then we parted — me toward sickbay, her toward trouble disguised as moisturizer and blackout answers.

The worst part was, I knew hers was the more dangerous path.

***

After Hy left for the med bay, the cabin felt too small. I trusted him to hold his own, but I wasn't incredibly keen on separating again. The engine hum pressed against my ears, the artwork pressed against my patience, and the urge to claw at my own arms pressed against every remaining scrap of decorum. I adjusted my shawl one more time, then gave up. It did nothing to hide the pink blotches. The calamine had dried to a chalky sheen that sat on my skin in uneven patches.

I stepped into the corridor anyway.

The first couple I passed stared. The woman's eyes went from my face to my forearms and back again. The man's gaze lingered a little too long on the rash near my jaw. I pressed my lips together.

I did not understand the fascination. I was walking on my own two feet. I had not trailed IV tubing behind me. I had not sprouted extra limbs. I was simply pink.

Another group of passengers rounded the bend, voices high from recent drama and free cocktails. Their chatter dipped for a moment when they saw me. One woman's mouth formed a silent "oh."

I kept my chin level. If they wanted a show, they could attend Mystery Night. My condition was uncomfortable, not apocalyptic.

Inwardly, I made a small adjustment. Perhaps I understood why some of our more dramatic patrons at the library became so prickly when people stared at their bandages or medical boots. Visibility did strange things to pride.

I took a turn toward the quieter section of the deck, the one Hy had gestured toward earlier when he mentioned crew areas. Signs for "Staff Only" began to appear. My arms itched. My temper itched too.

"I do not have plague," I muttered under my breath. "If I had something catastrophic, I would have stayed in my cabin out of courtesy."

A passing teenager snorted. Perhaps I had spoken louder than intended. I did not apologize.

I squared my shoulders and continued on, determined

to find calamine, answers, and at least one person on this ship who would speak to my face instead of my rash.

The farther I walked, the fewer passengers I saw. Carpet gave way to more utilitarian flooring. The lighting shifted to a flatter, workmanlike glow. A faint scent of detergent and warm metal replaced the perfume and spilled champagne from the public decks.

I knew that crew quarters existed behind the doors marked "Staff Only." I also knew passengers were encouraged to pretend those doors led straight into a magical void. Unfortunately for the *Photuris*, I had retired from public compliance years ago.

I tried to follow the mental map I had built from the ship directory and my own wandering. A left turn at the service lift, a right at the linen closet, then straight ahead toward the lower crew corridor. That had been the theory.

In practice, I found myself in an alcove lined with stacked banquet chairs.

I stopped, scowled at them for existing in the wrong place, then backtracked. Another attempt carried me to a wall of folded event signage. My arms burned. My patience thinned.

"I have navigated multi-floor record rooms," I told the wall quietly. "I have survived budget meetings. I refuse to be defeated by one floating hotel."

I stepped out again and almost collided with a young man in a black polo and headset. He carried a coil of cable over one shoulder and walked with the particular tired gait of someone who had dealt with both actors and electrical equipment.

"Sorry," he said automatically, then took in my appearance in full. His gaze paused on my blotches. "Whoa. That is a bold color story."

"It is a medical necessity," I replied. "I appear to be allergic to ferns."

He blinked, then gave a short laugh. "Mystery Night claims another victim."

I seized the opportunity. "You were part of that event, then."

"Lighting," he said, tapping his headset. "I am the one who makes the fake thunder and dramatic blackouts behave." His shoulders drooped a little. "At least, that is the goal."

Perfect. I was no longer lost. I had reached information.

"Convenient," I said. "I was hoping to find someone who understands tonight's blackout. The timing seemed… off."

He rolled his eyes toward the ceiling. "Tell me about it. I had the sequence fine-tuned. Cue, line, music, bump to half, then blackout. We rehearsed it three times."

"And yet," I prompted.

"And yet an hour before curtain, Laila sweeps in." He lifted his hands in a little theatrical flourish as he said her name. "Says one of the audience plants needs more time for a quick change in the wings. New cue. Lights out during Langley's dramatic line instead of the original moment. I redo the programming. I barely sit down before she changes the order of the crowd prompts too."

His frustration felt honest, the sort that comes from someone who likes systems and watched them get rearranged by committee.

"Did you tell security about the change," I asked.

He frowned. "Security? No. I told Laila she needed to clear it with them. I mean, they like to know when we are about to plunge a room full of paying guests into darkness." He shrugged one shoulder. "Once the knife came out and the blood started, she bugged out pretty fast. I did not see her near the officers at all."

That detail slid neatly into place beside what I had already seen. Her washed hands. Her flinch when Monty fussed about appearances. It did not condemn her. It did not clear her either.

The tech shifted the cable on his shoulder. "Then there was that mountain guy."

"Mountain," I repeated.

"Big fella," he said. "Island shirt, storm cloud face, stomach made of glass. He sat near the buffet. The second the blackout hit, he went pale. Full green around the edges. As soon as the lights came up, he tried to stand and missed his own feet."

"Makena Pali," I said.

"That his name? I called him Mauna Loa in my head." The tech grimaced at the memory. "He lost the crab rangoon behind the side curtain. Everywhere. Laila tried to get him a bucket, but his aim was enthusiastic instead of accurate."

Which explained her absence from security later and the hand washing. She had not been fleeing guilt. She had been fleeing bodily fluids.

For the moment, at least, that was the most reasonable conclusion.

The tech shook his head, then continued. "You would not believe the things you see working on a ship. People faint at karaoke. Proposals go sideways. One man thought a conga line was a good place for deep personal reflection. But that guy?" He jerked a thumb back toward the dining deck. "That was brutal. The way he was swaying, I am amazed he did not topple straight into the chocolate fountain."

"So, he was ill before the attack," I clarified. "Before Langley screamed about his pancreas."

"Absolutely. He had that far away stare people get when the room moves too much. I have seen it on smaller boats." The tech's mouth twisted. "Poor guy could not hold down a buffet on a ship this size. I do not know how he expects to handle that speedboat."

I latched onto the new word. "Speedboat."

"Oh. Yeah." The tech brightened a little, pleased to have an extra tidbit. "After the show, when everyone was still buzzing, I passed him near the service stairs. He was on his phone. Thought I was out of earshot. Said he had a reservation for a private launch in Nassau. Sent whoever it was his cabin number and everything. Pretty sure I heard him say he wanted to get off before the rest of the herd."

I tucked that into my mental file. Pali. Seasick. Wash of crab rangoon. Private speedboat at the next port. A man miserable on the Photuris, aching to trade one set of waves for another. It made little sense from a comfort perspective. From an escape perspective, it made far more.

"Thank you," I said. "That is very helpful."

He gave a small bow that might have once belonged to a community theater curtain call. "Any time. Always good to help someone who survived floral combat."

As he walked on, I considered what he had given me. Laila had changed the blackout cue with a seemingly reasonable explanation. Pali had been visibly, violently ill. Neither fact cleared either of them from suspicion. Yet both pushed the picture toward something more complicated than a simple villain in a darkened room.

My arms prickled. My thoughts did also. I set both sensations aside and focused on my immediate goal.

I still needed Laila. And calamine. Preferably in that order.

Finding crew quarters required equal parts stubbornness and selective disregard for signage. After the lighting tech pointed out a general direction with his cable, I followed a short flight of stairs past a storage alcove, skirted a cleaning cart, and ignored a politely worded notice about restricted access.

The air grew cooler as I moved deeper into the staff corridor. Voices echoed from behind closed doors. Laughter here, a burst of music there, the low murmur of people on a break from serving hundreds of passengers who believed the ship existed solely for their amusement.

A young woman in a housekeeping uniform stepped out of a linen room ahead of me. Her arms were piled high with folded towels. She stopped short when she saw me, eyes widening at the sight of my calamine stripes.

"I am not contagious," I assured her. "I trespass, but I do not infect."

Her mouth twitched. "You should not be back here,

ma'am."

"I know," I said. "However, I am on an urgent quest for both information and topical relief. Can you tell me where I might find Laila, your event coordinator?"

The housekeeper shifted her load. "Her cabin is further down, near the staff lounge. Third door on the right after the vending machine. Off limits to passengers." She hesitated, then added in a conspiratorial tone, "Just promise you will not tell Captain Monty I sent you. That man is wound very tight."

"I have noticed," I said. "Your secret is safe with me."

As she vanished back into her linen kingdom, I continued along the corridor. Carpet ended entirely. Bare flooring carried every step forward. I passed the vending machine, glowing softly in the dimmer light, then counted doors.

One. Two.

My arm protested again. I resisted the urge to scratch. Rash or no rash, I had reached the point of no return.

Third door on the right.

A small plaque bore Laila's name.

I paused long enough to draw a steadying breath. Calamine itched on my skin. Questions itched under it. The moisturizer in my tote felt heavier than it should have, a small reminder that nothing about this cruise remained simple.

Then I raised my hand and knocked.

Whatever waited on the other side, it would not be nearly as straightforward as extra calamine and a friendly chat.

CHAPTER SIXTEEN

I had unraveled organized crime syndicates, solved cases on nothing more than a half-smoked cigarette butt found in a storm drain, and figured out the bleary riddles of Medicare Part C. I could figure out a damned ship schematic.

That was the theory.

The *Photuris* said otherwise.

The carpeting swallowed sound with a plush smugness, and each intersection offered three possible wrong turns. Fluorescent sconces washed the corridor in warm hotel gold, too cheerful for a man sweating through a navigation problem he refused to call a navigation problem. Every few minutes, the faint vibration underfoot shifted, the engine's pulse rolling through the soles of my shoes. A reminder that the metal beast beneath me had more levels than common sense.

Passengers shuffled past, armed with sunhats and umbrella drinks, giving side-eyes I chose not to acknowledge. If anyone asked, I was surveying infrastructure. That sounded official enough.

When I finally found the polished stainless-steel sign reading **MEDICAL**, it gleamed under the overhead lights as though mocking me. I stepped inside, letting the antiseptic tang settle into my sinuses. Clean. Metallic. Unwelcoming.

A nurse lifted her gaze from a tablet. Her bun was tight enough to breach hull integrity.

"Can I help you?"

"Yeah," I said. "I'm here to see Langley."

"Absolutely not."

The air conditioner hummed. I dug into my pocket for my badge.

"I just need a few minutes," I said.

"He needs rest. Visitors are limited." Her voice carried the clipped efficiency of someone who had already turned away three drunk passengers and a man with a jellyfish sting today.

I opened my badge. Its metal edges caught the overhead light, a sharp glint that gave her pause.

"You're… law enforcement?"

"Was," I said. "Long enough to tell when someone's trying to silence a federal agent. Now let me in."

A muscle in her jaw twitched. "Five minutes. And keep your voice low."

She gestured toward a curtained alcove, shoes whispering across the vinyl floor as she stepped away. The med bay hummed softly with monitors, distant clinking metal, and the faint hiss of oxygen lines.

"You don't happen to have any calamine lotion lying around, do you?" I called after her. "I, uh, have a friend who had a tussle with a Boston fern."

"I'll see what we have."

The curtains rustled as I approached Langley's bed. The blue glow of his monitors painted thin shadows across his face. He looked drained, the kind of drained that settles in deep.

I pulled up a chair. It complained under my weight.

"Evening," I said. "Thought you'd appreciate some facts before your painkillers finish eating your brain."

He swallowed, grimacing at the motion. The ship's hum vibrated through the bedframe, turning his pain into a faint audible tremor.

"You found something?" he whispered.

"Couple somethings," I said. The curtain shifted slightly from an unseen draft. "First one? Alicia Bart. She was your whistleblower. She admitted it. All she wanted was time to move her own assets before the whole Centurion circus collapsed."

Langley groaned. The monitor beeped in sympathetic distress. I kept an ear on the approaching footsteps beyond the curtain.

"I should have frozen everything..." His voice rasped through dried-out regret. "God. I knew it. I knew if I froze his accounts, it would spook him. And I needed the whole operation, not just Bart."

"Yeah, well," I said, keeping my tone low, "you know what they say about assuming."

His eyes tightened. A pulse flickered visibly in his throat.

"I'm never going to find out who his partner is now. I'm never going to recover the money. Some of the folks he scammed? That was their life savings."

"I know where a million of it is."

His head jerked in a tiny, startled motion.

"What?"

"Your boy Pali. He's got one million in ten-grand bricks. Cash. Neat as a banker's smile."

The monitor leapt again, a frantic metronome.

"What else?" he whispered.

"So," Langley whispered, "you think Pali's the one who stabbed me?"

The question rippled through the room. The ventilation unit issued a low hum. His shoulders shook.

"Hey," I said. "Easy. I think he's more focused on abandoning ship. We've got intel he's planning to make a run for it in Nassau."

The color drained from his face.

"You can't let him do that!" His voice pitched upward, ragged. "If Pali bolts, I don't have a snowball's chance of making my case. I've got to call my superiors! I've got to go after him!"

He yanked at his pulse ox. The wire snapped free with a digital chirp. His IV line tugged dangerously. The sheets twisted around his legs.

The curtain whipped open.

"Absolutely not!" the nurse barked. She strode in, her shoes pounding the vinyl. "Sir, lie back down. You're going to tear out your line!"

"He's endangering—"

She silenced him by injecting something clear into his IV port. The reaction was instant. His limbs loosened. His eyes blurred. He sagged back against the pillows with an offended exhale.

"You… can't… sedate… a federal…"

"That's above my pay grade," she said. Her tone could have sanded wood. "Detective Reynolds, out."

I opened my mouth, but her glare carried the force of a taser.

She shoved a bottle of calamine lotion into my hand. "Go."

So, I went.

The med bay door hissed shut behind me, sealing in the antiseptic chill. I stood alone in the corridor where the fluorescent lights hummed overhead and the carpeting swallowed every footstep.

I turned the calamine bottle in my hand, the plastic warm from her grip and mine. Langley was out cold. Pali was ready to cut loose. Alicia Bart was halfway through a disappearing act.

I tucked the lotion into my pocket. The weight settled against my hip.

"Hang on, kid," I muttered, glancing back once at the closed door. "We'll keep the wheels turning."

Then I started down the corridor, the ship humming beneath me, its endless hallways stretching forward like a puzzle someone spilled on purpose.

Time to find Eugenia. And pray she hadn't wandered into trouble with anything greener than her.

***

Laila opened the door almost before my knuckles left the wood. Her eyes looked tired around the edges, the way staff eyes often did after a long night of pretending everything was fine in public spaces.

"Eugenia? Are you alright?"

Topical humiliation was one thing. Pride was another.

"Currently half dusted in calamine and half on fire," I said. "Hy's supply ran out. I was hoping you might have some. Emergency stash for unfortunate guests who lose fistfights with ferns."

Her gaze skimmed my arms, then my cheek. A tiny wince tugged at the corner of her mouth.

"Oh, poor you. Come in."

Her quarters felt smaller than I had expected. The ceiling seemed lower than the passenger decks, and the walls carried the faint hum of the ship's machinery under the paint. The air smelled of citrus cleaner, a hint of lavender, and something warm that reminded me of roasted nuts.

The bed was neatly made, blanket tight, corners sharp. A tiny desk by the porthole held a planner, a row of color-coded pens, and an empty tea mug. A narrow wardrobe door stood ajar, showing a curtain of pressed uniforms in careful order.

On the tiny counter beside a compact sink sat a few personal objects that did not belong to the ship at all.

"I am sorry to bother you," I said, stepping further in. "Hy said you might rescue me before I shed my own skin."

She closed the door and leaned on it for a second, as though bracing herself before moving again.

"If anyone deserves rescue tonight, it is you," she said. "I will look. I must have something."

Her voice shook more than my rash warranted.

While she rummaged under the sink, I let my eyes wander. Old habit. A lifetime around books and people taught me that shelves and nightstands often told more truth than the mouths that owned them.

A framed photograph stood next to the tea mug. I stepped closer.

Warm sunlight flooded a modest kitchen in that frozen moment. A younger Laila grinned at the camera, cheeks full, hair tucked behind one ear. Beside her stood an older woman in a printed apron, arm wrapped around Laila's shoulders, eyes crinkled at the corners. Flour dusted the counter behind them. A pot simmered on the stove. The frame edges were slightly worn, as though fingers had traced them often.

"Who's this?" I asked.

I did not turn right away. I could feel her reaction in the silence. The air tightened around us.

"My Nonna."

Her voice thinned around the word.

Next to the photograph, a wine bottle stood near the sink. Nearby, half hidden behind the mug, a single wooden chopstick lay forgotten, its lacquer chipped at one end.

Only one. I filed that away.

How did one eat with only one chopstick?

My gaze dropped to a small ceramic bowl near the corner. At first glance, I assumed potpourri or snack mix. As I leaned closer, the contents shifted under the light. Fine reddish-brown grit clustered in small piles, studded with tiny shard shapes that could have been fragments of pits or shells.

It looked like coffee grounds but smelled faintly of almond and something darker, almost bitter.

"Oh! I'm so embarrassed," Laila said quickly.

Her hand arrived before mine did, sliding the bowl gently out of reach. The movement was careful, almost reverent. Her fingers trembled as she set it nearer the sink.

"I have been meaning to clean that up," she added. "Nonna used to make her Amarena syrup every Sunday," she said, touching the rim of the bowl with a small, fond smile. "I tried making a little earlier. I was using her old method… wine bottle, chopstick. Helps pit the cherries. The smell helps me feel near her, even when she's… not. Only problem is, I'm such a mess, the sugar usually gets everywhere. Nonna used to always fuss."

My eyes roved the counter. No sugar.

Well, she'd managed to clean up something.

"Your Nonna looks lovely," I said, lifting the frame with both hands. The glass felt cool and smooth under my fingers. "She has that rare expression that says the kitchen belongs to her, but anyone hungry is welcome."

Laila laughed once, a short sound that cracked in the middle. She took a step toward me. Her eyes shone more than the overhead light could justify.

"She raised me," Laila said. "My parents died in a car crash when I was eight. One minute we were all together, the next there was only her and me and a tiny house that always smelled of basil."

I nodded and set the frame down again, a fraction of an inch closer to her side of the counter. She reached out, steadying it with a thumb.

"She taught me everything good," Laila continued. "How to stir sauce without scorching it. How to find the sweetest tomatoes. How to laugh on days when bills came in a pile. I thought she would live forever." Her jaw tightened. "Old women with strong hands always seem permanent until they are not."

The room felt smaller. The ship hummed through the floor under my shoes. Somewhere beyond the walls, passengers clinked glasses and went about their oblivious evenings.

"What happened?" I asked gently.

"The usual story," she said. "Age. A fall. Then a care facility that promised the world and delivered the minimum. Sadly, it was all she could afford." She paused, a sour look flitting across her features. I knew that look. That's why I keep a roll of antacids in my purse at all times.

I offered an understanding nod. "Social Security isn't what it used to be."

"No, no. More like bad investments. Anyway, I tried to visit every chance I had between cruises. I tried to make her comfortable, but it simply wasn't her home. Pretty sure she died of a broken heart." Her breath hitched. "The night she died, I was here on this ship, smiling through a theme trivia contest. I missed the call. By the time I got a signal for my phone again, it was already over."

Her hand brushed the frame again, thumb tracing the edge.

"I have been trying to make that up to her ever since,"

she whispered.

The bowl of almond-scented crumbs sat within reach of her other hand. She avoided it carefully.

Grief sat in that small room with us, crowded in between the citrus cleaner and the lavender.

I let the quiet settle for a few breaths before I tugged at the other thread tugging at my brain.

"Laila," I said, keeping my voice mild, "the lighting technician mentioned something. He said you asked for a last-minute cue change before Mystery Night. He also said you told Captain Monty it was his error."

Her shoulders rose, then fell. She notched her gaze away from me, toward the tiny porthole and the black water beyond.

"I did," she said. "I was just afraid to admit it to Captain Monty. He can be so exacting." The word carried a heavier meaning. Punishing. Unforgiving.

"You told him the blackout misfire was the technician's fault," I said. "Meanwhile you adjusted the cue so one of your planted guests could manage a costume change."

"I know I should not have blamed him," she said. "It was my call. I thought I had every beat under control. I thought I could handle one shift in the script."

Her mouth twisted. "Then the knife appeared. And the blood. And everyone started yelling. Monty looked at me as if I had opened a trapdoor under the entire evening. I panicked."

"You panicked," I repeated. "So, you shielded yourself first."

"Yes," she said. "Because I cannot afford to lose this

job."

Her eyes finally met mine. They held the same desperate shine I had seen on patrons at the library who could not pay their fines but refused to give up their books.

"I still have mortgage payments on my Nonna's house," she said. "The house I grew up in. It is all I have left of her that does not fit in a frame. If I lose this job, I lose that house. I lose... *her*. I cannot risk it."

Her gaze drifted to the photograph, then to the moved bowl, then back to me.

She balanced on a very narrow ledge. Duty on one side. Survival on the other.

I could not tell yet which direction she leaned.

"I am not here to cost you your job, dear," I said, patting her hand. "Or your house. I am here because someone tried to kill a man under your event lighting, and I do not enjoy unsolved puzzles."

Her shoulders sagged in relief and tension at the same time.

"I have calamine," she quickly replied, as if grateful for a subject that involved only skin. She opened a small cabinet above the sink and pulled out a nearly full bottle. "I keep it for mosquito bites. You can take it."

I accepted the bottle, turning it in my hands. The label peeled slightly at the corner. My arms already itched in anticipation of relief.

"Thank you," I said. "For this. And for your honesty."

She nodded, but her gaze slid past me again to the bowl she had moved. Her fingers brushed the counter near it, then pulled back.

I let my eyes rest on it one more time. The reddish grit. The tiny shard shapes. "Leftovers from a snack," I repeated mildly.

She lifted her chin. "I will throw them out after you leave. Please don't let anyone know I'm secretly a slob."

"Mums the word." I smiled and locked my lips tight and threw away the key.

I tucked the calamine into my tote next to the suspiciously heavy moisturizer Hy had stolen, then stepped toward the door.

"Laila," I said, hand on the knob, "for what it is worth, grief often makes people choose poorly in the moment. That does not mean they are beyond saving."

Her eyes glistened again. She nodded once.

I stepped out into the corridor, the calamine bottle tucked into my tote and the cool air brushing my still blotchy skin. My arms burned less. My thoughts burned more.

I had come for lotion. I walked away with far more than relief for a rash.

A bowl of gritty crumbs that smelled faintly of almonds but could have been any number of culinary experiments. A wine bottle with streaks that might have been syrup. A single wooden chopstick with no partner. And a young woman carrying enough grief to fill the tiny room behind me.

None of it formed a picture. Not yet.

But it all sat together in my head, shifting around, looking for edges that matched.

I adjusted the strap on my tote and started toward the passenger decks. My skin still tingled under the calamine's cool veil, and every step reminded me how ridiculous I must have looked earlier, covered in rash and dignity in equal proportion.

Still, even with the sting fading, something unsettled lingered. Not sharp enough to name. Not bright enough to shine a warning. Just… present.

I told myself I was being dramatic.
I had, after all, nearly lost a fight with a fern.

But as I walked on, giving a polite nod to a passing steward who absolutely stared too long at my pink-spotted neckline, I knew one thing for certain.

I had not wasted the evening.

And whatever happened next, Laila was no longer just a smiling cruise director in a well-tailored uniform.

She was a person with layers. And layers always revealed something.

Eventually.

CHAPTER SEVENTEEN

By the time the *Photuris* eased into Nassau, the whole ship buzzed with that particular brand of vacation frenzy that made sane people elbow each other for towel animals. I stood with Eugenia at the rail on **Deck 5**, watching the tenders bob and sway as they ferried passengers toward shore. The sun hit the water in hard coins of light. Heat rose off the waves in lazy, confident curls.

Our target towered three passengers ahead in the debarkation line.

Makena Pali looked worse than the last time I saw him. He had the color of week-old lettuce and the posture of a man braced for either a firing squad or a buffet. One hand clamped on the rail. The other held his stomach as though he were afraid it might jump ship without him.

"He really does look like a six-foot-eight Kermit," Eugenia murmured at my shoulder.

"Green around the gills," I said. "I will never forgive

you for making me picture that."

The line shuffled forward. Crew members chirped about sunscreen and last tender times. The air smelled of sunblock, diesel, and anticipation. I ran my eyes over the dock, mapping exits and blind spots out of habit. A café sat just beyond the tourist kiosks, bright umbrellas shouting in primary colors. The rest of town spilled out behind it in narrow streets, pastel buildings, and the patient predation of souvenir shops.

We followed Pali down the tender ramp with what I liked to think of as casual stealth. Dark sunglasses, nondescript shirts, and the shambling pace of people who had nowhere better to be. I tucked my badge wallet into my pocket. Old reflex. No legal weight out here, but it made me feel less naked.

"He is going to bolt," Eugenia said under her breath as we stepped onto the dock. Heat hit us full in the face, thick and humid.

"That is the plan," I said. "Question is whether we can use it."

Ahead, Pali paused on the pier, swaying slightly. A crew member pointed him toward town. He lumbered forward, one giant man in a sea of floral prints and floppy hats.

I nudged Eugenia gently. "Stay close. Stay boring. No waving your tote around like a semaphore."

"I do not wave," she sniffed. "I signal with purpose."

"Signal quieter," I said, and we slipped into the tide of passengers, letting the island swallow us whole.

Nassau town center had that polished port feel. Fresh paint, clean sidewalks, shops poised to siphon cash from people in wet sandals. Pali moved through it all with the stiff determination of a man trying not to lose his breakfast on a postcard.

We kept about half a block back, ducking behind a cluster of cruise people every time he slowed. I pretended to study a map posted near a jewelry store while watching his reflection in the glass.

"You mentioned a bowl," I said, keeping my voice low.

"Cherry pits. Funny how they smell like almonds when you crush them." Eugenia walked beside me, hat brim pulled down, blotches mostly hidden. "Girl's not much of a housekeeper, if I'm being honest. At least she managed to wipe up the sugar."

"Sugar?"

"Recipe calls for a healthy portion of it. Said her Nonna made Amarena syrup every Sunday. Used to fuss at her for getting it everywhere. Losing her seems like it was really a blow for Laila."

"Died in her own house?" I asked.

"No. A home."

I shivered at the word. I pulled at my collar.

"Couldn't afford private care. Seems like she made a few bad money choices. Ultimately, sounds like she died of a broken heart."

Saying it out loud, it felt like a cautionary tale. I tried to shake off the gloom.

We crossed a side street. The smell of frying seafood and sweet rum drifted past. Somewhere a steel drum band tried valiantly to make "Hotel California" sound tropical.

"What about the cue change?" I asked.

"She admitted it," Eugenia said. "Said she panicked and blamed the lighting tech because she cannot afford to lose the job. She still pays mortgage on her Nonna's house."

"Hm," I scratch the thin grit of stubble peppered across my chin. "She lies to save herself, but she also gives you calamine for free." I nodded once before I continued. "Contradictions. Good. I like people complicated. Means we cannot write them off too soon."

Somewhere a steel drum band tried valiantly to make "Hotel California" sound tropical.

I held my arm across Eugenia's chest, pausing to let a group of tourists pose with a man dressed as a pirate. Pali lumbered past them and turned toward the brightly colored café I had clocked from the rail. He hesitated at the entrance as if building courage, then ducked under the awning and disappeared inside.

"There," I said. "Café. Shade. And relief for my prostate." I jerked my chin. "Perfect for progress or crime."

"Or both," Eugenia said.

We crossed the street together, blending with a cluster of passengers in loud shirts. My knees felt every step. My head felt the weight of Langley's case. The island sun threw everything into sharp relief. Somewhere in the middle of it, a man with a stomach full of regret and a pocket full of stolen cash was about to make a move.

We just had to be close enough to hear it.

The café spilled out onto the sidewalk in a sprawl of painted tables and mismatched chairs. A faded chalkboard by the entrance listed specials in careful lettering: jerk chicken, plantain fritters, something involving conch that sounded illegal in three states.

Inside, ceiling fans turned lazily. The air smelled of lime, fried onions, and cold beer. A radio played low behind the bar.

We spotted Pali in the back, sitting at a table near the window. He sat with his back to the wall, eyes on the door, one leg jiggling. A glass of something clear and sweating sat untouched in front of him.

I steered Eugenia toward a table two down from his, angled so we could see without being obvious. My knees cracked when I sat. Hers did not, but only because she was better at pretending.

A waiter appeared in record time, all smiles and professional enthusiasm. "Welcome, my friends! You here from the ship?"

"We are just looking at the menu," I said, picking it up as a shield.

The menu listed ten things I recognized and five I did not. The waiter did not move.

"Everything here is fresh," he assured us. "Very authentic. Very local. I recommend ordering now. We get busy when the tenders land."

"We might not stay long," I tried.

He smiled wider. "Then you will want something quick. A salad? The soup of the day? Very hearty. Very traditional."

Across the room, the bell over the door jingled. Alicia Bart slipped inside with the caution of someone who expected to be followed. She wore oversized sunglasses and a sundress that probably cost more than my first car. Her hair was pulled back tight. Her eyes scanned the room once, sharp and restless.

She saw Pali. He lifted one hand. She moved toward him.

"Hy," Eugenia breathed.

"Menu up," I muttered. "Eyes down. Ears open."

The waiter cleared his throat expectantly. He had no interest in being cast as background scenery.

"Fine," I said. "Salad for the lady. And I'll have…" I scanned the menu, landed on the only soup listed, and regretted my life. "Cow Cod Soup."

"Excellent choice," he beamed. "You want it spicy?"

"I want it not to kill me."

He laughed, scribbled, and whisked away before I could change my mind.

Eugenia leaned in. "Cow cod?" she whispered.

"It's probably like surf and turf. Bahamian-style," I said.

"Are you sure?" she asked, her wide-brimmed hat probably pulling in signals from Skynet.

I chose to ignore her and focused on the table behind her instead.

Alicia slid into the chair across from Pali with practiced poise. Up close, her tan looked thinner. Her mouth held more tension than gloss. She took off her sunglasses and set them on the table with a decisive click.

"You look terrible," she said without preamble.

"You would too if the floor kept trying to kiss you," Pali muttered. His voice carried just enough to reach us over the murmur of the café.

I tilted my head, presenting one ear toward them while pretending to study the condensation on my water glass.

"Where is it?" Alicia asked.

He stared at her. Sweat glistened at his hairline. "Where's what?"

She waved a small, impatient hand. "I do not care about the million. That is chump change compared to what that drive is worth."

"Drive?" Eugenia whispered.

I shushed her without looking. "Napkin," I murmured, sliding one toward her as cover.

Pali scrubbed his hands over his face. "I told you, I couldn't find it."

"So, you stole his cash instead," she said. "Classy."

"I am taking the million and getting the hell outta Dodge," he growled. "If you are smart, you will too."

She leaned back, eyes narrowing. The sunlight from the window drew a hard edge along her profile. "No. If I leave, the first thing Langley and those snooping seniors are going to do is point the finger at me."

I felt Eugenia's eyes flick toward me at that. I did not return the look. The "snooping seniors" sat silently and soaked it in.

"Honestly, you are doing me a favor by pulling up stakes," Alicia went on. "Keep the million. You just better hope I do not find out you are holding out on me and keeping that drive for yourself. I am not stupid. It shows where everything is, and I am running out of time to move it."

She tapped one nail against the table. "The stabbing

200

stalled Langley, but it is only a matter of time before he grows a brain and freezes the assets."

My gut tightened. She said it cleanly, without a hint of guilt. Practical. Cold. The type of cold I recognized from too many interview rooms.

Pali glanced at the door. "I have a boat to catch," he said. "Private launch. I am done with this floating circus."

I keyed in on that word — *private*. The old wheels started churning.

"Then go," Alicia said, lifting her chin. "But if you are lying to me about that drive, I will make sure you are not the only one stranded."

He pushed back his chair. It scraped the tile with a harsh squeal. For a man half sick and full of stolen money, he moved faster than I liked. He headed for the door, pausing only long enough to ask the host in a low voice for directions to some local marina. Nassau Harbor Club Marina.

"That's over at Paradise Island," the host replied.

My pulse picked up.

"Hy — " Eugenia started.

"I know," I said.

We watched him disappear into the bright slice of street beyond.

My first instinct was to throw some cash on the table and follow him. Old muscle memory. Suspect walking. Shadows lengthening.

Eugenia's hand closed around my wrist under the table. Her grip was firmer than her voice.

"Before you go charging into a marina like a bargain-rate bounty hunter," she said quietly, "consider his stomach."

"His stomach?"

"He has spent most of this cruise looking like a six foot eight Kermit the Frog," she said. "Green around the gills. Listless. On Mystery Night, he could barely stand. The lighting technician said he went fully ill the moment the blackout hit. He was already halfway to the Crab Rangoon apocalypse before Langley cried out."

I remembered the retching — the sound echoing off the tiny bathroom tiles while I rifled through his room. The pallor. The sweat. The way he clutched the rail on the tender earlier as though the sea wanted him personally.

"Are you saying he could not have stabbed Langley in that blackout?"

"I am saying seasickness does not care about your murderous ambitions," she replied. "He might have had motive. He might have had money. But I do not think he had balance. I hate to say it, but Alicia Bart and her seventy-five-dollar lipstick may have pulled the wool over my eyes."

I let that settle. It fit what I had seen. It did not clear him of theft or conspiracy. It tipped the scales away from him as our knife-wielding phantom.

"And Bart's drink?" I asked. "You think he poisoned that?"

"Between clinging to the rail and painting the ship with seafood, when would he have had the opportunity? And, if you'll remember, the pool boy saw Alicia arguing with Bart and getting quite upset when Bart's drink was overturned before he had a chance to sip from it," she reasoned. "No. Pali is dirty, but I do not think he is our killer. I think Mrs. Bart, there, may have pulled the proverbial wool over my eyes."

I exhaled slowly. "What are you saying? We let him walk?"

Her eyes flashed. "We do not have to let him vanish. We simply choose how."

She had a point. Several. I dug my phone out of my pocket and turned slightly in my chair, shielding it with the menu.

Eugenia leaned closer, her voice barely moving the air between us. "Who are you calling?"

I didn't look at her. "Bahamian police."

"Can they hold him for theft aboard the ship?"

I shook my head. "Not to arrest him."

Her brow furrowed. "Then why?"

"Because I don't need him arrested," I said. "I need him *stalled.*"

"That's a distinction without much comfort," she murmured.

"No," I said. "It's the only distinction that matters."

I shifted my cup a half inch, using the movement to shield my mouth.

"Right now, we can't get him for theft. We weren't supposed to be in Bart's room, and I sure as hell wasn't supposed to be in Pali's. Anything turned up there is smoke, not fire."

"But you *saw* the money."

"I did," I said. "And legally, it means nothing."

She inhaled through her nose. "Then what are you counting on?"

"Customs," I said. "And panic."

Her eyes sharpened. "Explain."

"He walks into a foreign port carrying a fortune and tries to leave on a private speedboat without declaring it, somebody's going to ask questions. They don't need a warrant. They don't need a victim. They just need a man acting nervous with too much cash."

"And the whole financial scheme?"

"That's Langley's lane," I said. "Not mine."

She hesitated. "Langley's unconscious."

"Which is why I'm buying him time," I said. "If Pali bolts now, Langley never gets a clean shot at him. If he's detained, even briefly, Langley wakes up and asks the right questions."

Eugenia went still. "You're hoping Pali still has the partnership papers."

"I'm hoping he hasn't taken the time to destroy them."

"And if he did?" she asked.

I finally looked at her then. "Then we learn just how badly he's afraid of what's written on that paper."

She stared at me for a long moment.

"This is a gamble," she said.

I lifted my cup. "Every case is."

"Use what we can, then," she suggested.

"Use what we can," I agreed.

When the Bahamian police dispatcher picked up, I pitched my voice calmer than I felt and gave them the basics. Anonymous tip. Passenger heading for a Nassau Harbour Club Marina — Paradise Island — with roughly one million in undeclared cash. Physical description. No mention of knives or federal investigators.

"We will kick it over to port security, sir," the voice on the line promised. "Thank you."

I hung up, thumb lingering on the screen for a second.

"There," I said. "He might not be our killer, but we can at least keep him from spending that money on Cuban cigars either."

"Practical justice," Eugenia said. "Very you."

The waiter reappeared, balancing a tray. He slid a plate with a respectable salad in front of Eugenia, then set a steaming bowl in front of me. The broth was cloudy. Something pale and fleshy floated in the center.

I stared at it. The investigation had just taken a turn into truly uncharted territory.

"What is this?" I asked.

"Your Cow Cod Soup, sir," the waiter said.

I pointed at the offending object in the middle. "That is neither cow nor cod. What is floating in the middle of that bowl?"

"Bull penis, sir," he replied pleasantly.

Across from me, Eugenia inhaled at the wrong time and sprayed a fine mist of water across the table.

Alicia Bart's head snapped in our direction.

And just like that, things got interesting again.

***

If anyone ever asked, I would insist the water attack was involuntary.

"Bull penis," the waiter had said, entirely too calmly. The words pierced my composure at the same time Hy's eyebrows shot up toward his hairline.

Water went down the wrong pipe. Then it went everywhere else.

I clapped a napkin to my mouth, coughing and mortified. Hy blinked at me through droplets, his expression hovering somewhere between affronted and entertained.

"Sorry," I wheezed. "My body rejected the concept."

"Your body and I are in agreement," he said, eyeing the bowl as if it might try to climb out.

Alicia's chair scraped lightly against the floor. I saw her out of the corner of my eye as she rose. She reached for her bag with quick, controlled motions. No fumbling. No guilt. Just decision.

"She is leaving," I murmured, lowering my napkin.

Hy followed my line of sight. "Of course she is. We have that effect on people."

"She didn't see us," I hissed and stuck out a plump pink tongue.

We watched as she dropped a few bills on the table without waiting for change and headed for the exit, shoulders tense, chin high.

Hy threw a crumpled local bill on our own table. "Come on," he said. "Before our last potential suspect vanishes into a duty-free shop."

"What about your—"

"I am abandoning ship," he said firmly, standing. "Literally and figuratively."

I did not argue. Any further discussion of the soup would have sent me into a fresh coughing fit.

We slipped out after Alicia, the café's ceiling fans stirring the air behind us, the smell of lime and broth clinging to our clothes. Outside, the sun hit us full-on again, blinding for a second.

Alicia's dress flashed ahead in the crowd as she turned down a side path toward the beach, moving faster now that she had open space in front of her.

Hy fell into step beside me, his jaw set. "She did not even flinch when Pali admitted stealing the million," he said under his breath. "No shock. No outrage. Just… logistics."

"She already wrote that money off," I said. "She is focused on this mysterious drive."

"And on not being next in the investigative crosshairs," he added.

"Do you think I got it wrong?" I asked tentatively, suddenly worried that I'd misinterpreted the solarium conversation.

Hy offered no condemnation, nor comfort. "Just keep up."

We trailed her past a row of shops and a man renting oversized floats shaped like flamingos. Sand appeared underfoot in patches, kicked up by tourists heading to the water.

I adjusted the strap of my tote, feeling both calamine and curiosity prickle under my skin. Our shore excursion had become less about scenery and more about survival.

The sea spread ahead, blue and bright, as Alicia stepped onto the beach.

We followed.

The beach looked like someone had ordered it from a catalog labeled "Tropical Fantasy, Standard Package." Pale sand, turquoise water, palm trees arranged at flattering angles. Sunbathers had staked out territory with towels and inflatable toys. Children shrieked in the shallows. Someone out on a jet ski carved a white line across the blue.

Alicia did not pause to admire any of it. She made a beeline for a cluster of cabanas near the waterline, canvas shades fluttering slightly in the breeze.

Hy and I slowed, pretending to study a chalkboard menu listing frozen concoctions with irresponsible names. I angled my body so I could watch her reflection in the plastic display case. Once she settled, we followed.

The beach was doing its level best to look innocent.

White sand stretched out in every direction, smooth as sifted flour, broken only by rows of identical loungers and cabanas that promised rest, relaxation, and absolutely no felonies. The water beyond shimmered in impossible shades of blue, the kind that made brochures lie for a living. A steel drum band played somewhere to our left, cheerful enough to irritate a person who had not solved a crime.

Hy slowed, scanning the open stretch of sand with a look usually reserved for parking lots and crime scenes. "This looks good," I commented as I gestured to a spot on the beach.

"What do you expect me to do? Pull up a patch of sand and cop a squat?" he muttered.

"Don't be ridiculous," I said, already unshouldering my tote.

He eyed it suspiciously. "That bag weighs more than my grandkid."

"Preparation," I said. "Is not a character flaw."

I crouched and, with a practiced flick, unfurled a neatly folded blanket onto the sand. It landed flat, no fuss, no flapping corners. Next came a compact, collapsible sunshade that popped open with a soft mechanical sigh and anchored neatly into the sand. Two bottles of water followed, cold enough to sweat immediately. Then sunscreen.

I handed the bottle to Hy. "Skin cancer is no joke."

He grunted but took the bottle. Squeezed a cautious amount into his palm. Rubbed it into his forearms like he was handling something mildly radioactive.

From our low vantage point, the world shifted. We were no longer two seniors loitering suspiciously. We were beach people. Harmless. Hydrated. Properly SPF'd.

Hy lowered himself onto the blanket with a sound that suggested several joints filed formal complaints.

"I just want it on the record," he said, "I hate the beach."

"Noted." I leaned back on my elbows, eyes trained on the cabana.

Alicia adjusted her chair and turned a page in the book she'd pulled from her bag. Unhurried. Unbothered.

One of the cabana staff stepped up, a young man in a branded polo and the smile of someone whose income depended on tips and patience.

"Special today?" he chirped, holding up a tall glass with a paper umbrella and entirely too much garnish. "Rum punch on the house if you are from the cruise ship. Comes with cherries."

He said the last word with pride, as if cherries were a luxury.

Alicia recoiled as if he had offered her a live snake.

"Are you trying to kill me?" she snapped. "I am deathly allergic to cherries, you moron. I will blow up like that girl from Willy Wonka. Get those things away from me!"

Heads turned. The cabana boy's smile collapsed.

"I—I am so sorry, miss," he stammered, quickly pulling the drink back. "I did not know—"

"Of course you did not know," she said, breathing fast. "No one pays attention until someone stops breathing."

Her hand hovered near her throat, and I spotted the bracelet. The same bracelet I had seen on two separate occasions but did not fully register.

It was a medical-alert bracelet!

Of course! That's why it never seemed to match her designer outfits. I resisted the urge to smack myself in the forehead.

Alicia composed herself, exhaled sharply, and shook her head.

"Just get me something without fruit," she said, tone dropping. "Anything. Mineral water. Ice. That is it."

He nodded frantically and hurried away, as if the cherries themselves might pursue him.

Hy leaned closer to me, his voice a low growl. "Deathly allergic," he repeated. "To cherries."

"Yeah. Missed that," I admitted. My heart pumped faster, not from the sun, but from the pieces shifting quietly into place.

Alicia re-situated herself in the cabana, muttering under her breath. She dug through her bag, probably checking for an EpiPen. That kind of reaction did not sound hypothetical.

If Alicia could not be near cherries without puffing up, the idea of her handling a Bourbon Cherry Bomb behind the scenes lost its plausibility. "No way she dosed Bart's drink," I murmured. "She would have been the first one in distress."

Hy's eyes narrowed, following my gaze. "So, she is a vulture, not the poisoner."

"A survivor," I corrected. "Of a certain sort."

He grunted agreement.

The cabana boy returned with a bottle of water and a glass full of ice, no garnish in sight. Alicia took it with a curt nod, then sank onto the lounge chair, one hand pressed to her chest. Her shoulders sagged.

She did not look like a woman basking in ill-gotten gains. She looked like a woman dodging one disaster at a time.

We watched her sip cautiously at the water, shoulders slowly dropping from around her ears.

"So, we are left with a million stolen, a missing drive, a poisoned drink, a stabbing, and two suspects who are highly inconvenient but increasingly wrong for the central crimes," Hy said.

"In short," I agreed, "we are adrift."

A wave broke against the shore. My blotchy arms itched again under the heat. The calamine helped, but my skin still remembered the fern.

"I suppose we should be grateful," I suggested. "We came ashore hoping to cross at least one name off our list. It appears we have managed two."

"Grateful is not my primary emotion right now," Hy said. "I am leaning toward annoyed."

"Oh, believe me," I said. "My emotions are having quite a conference of their own."

He grunted. "I hate puzzles that lead nowhere."

"Then you chose the wrong cruise," I said.

We sat there a moment longer, two aging busybodies on a postcard beach, watching a woman who was infuriatingly not our killer. But it also left us with no alternative.

The light reflected off the water, turning everything into alternating blurs of gold and blue. Passengers laughed and shouted around us, blissfully unaware of stolen millions and poisoned cocktails. Their biggest concern seemed to be whether they had time for both shopping and snorkeling before all aboard.

I envied them for exactly six seconds.

"Langley is going to hate this update," Hy said quietly. "If he ever wakes up long enough to hear it."

"He will have to accept that reality does not bend to his case file," I said. "None of this is neat."

"Neat is for desk jobs," Hy said. "Murder never listens."

I glanced sideways at him. "Are you okay?"

"I am on an island watching my list of suspects evaporate," he said. "I am wearing sensible shoes. I am carrying a bottle of calamine and a federal investigation in my head. Define 'okay'."

"So, no," I said.

He huffed, which meant yes and no in equal measure.

We reached the edge of the port area, the ship rising in

front of us like a gleaming reminder that we were not done. Not even close.

On the tender ride back, I sat near the rail with my tote in my lap, the calamine bottle bumping gently against the stolen moisturizer. The boat rocked in a controlled, purposeful way. Pali would have hated it.

Hy sat beside me, one hand wrapped around the bench edge, the other around the strap of his bag. Salt air slicked his hair back a little. He looked tired. Stubborn. Entirely himself.

"What are you thinking?" I asked.

"That shore excursions are overrated," he replied. "And I may have to admit that maybe I'm losing my touch."

The island receded slowly behind us, its bright buildings shrinking into color blocks. The water between us and it shimmered, deceptively peaceful.

"We know more than we did this morning," I offered. "We know Pali is a thief with a weak stomach, not our stabber. We know Alicia is morally bankrupt and fruit-challenged, but not our poisoner. And we know there is a drive somewhere that it incredibly important." I paused, and my voice lost its momentum. "And we have absolutely no idea where it is."

The steel drum notes carried on the wind. We sat in silence for a moment. Finally, Hy stood up and angrily dusted caked sand from his person. I shielded my hand from the flying grains.

"I'm going back to the damned ship," he growled. I scrambled to collect my belongings and scuffled behind him as he stomped across the sand.

213

I was on land, but I had never felt more adrift in my life.

CHAPTER EIGHTEEN

The gangway thudded into place with a hollow clang that traveled up my legs and lodged behind my knees. *The Photuris* welcomed us back—too bright, too polished, pretending nothing ugly ever happened between ports. Crew smiled. Passengers shuffled past clutching duty-free bags and sunburned pride. The ship reeked of sunscreen and cooked skin.

Eugenia walked beside me, posture straight, eyes forward. We didn't talk. We didn't need to. The shore excursion had done exactly what none of us wanted—it ruled things out instead of narrowing them down.

Med bay lights glowed ahead, sterile and stubborn. The place had a way of looking the same no matter what went down inside it. Pain came and went. Answers didn't.

Langley lay propped up this time, not flat on his back like a felled tree. And he was conscious.

I might have felt less awkward if he'd still been passed out.

215

Color had crept back into the inspector's face, though he still looked like a man who'd lost an argument with gravity. A nurse hovered nearby, arms crossed, daring us to cause a scene.

"Well?" Langley said. His voice was steadier than I expected. That alone felt like an accusation.

I told him. All of it. Nassau. Pali. The café. Alicia. The drive that wasn't there. The money that was.

"I'd hoped to stall long enough for you to recover and question him. I left a message with Nurse Ratched over there in case you woke up."

Langley stared at the ceiling for a long second. Didn't blink. Didn't swear. Just let it land.

"Yeah. I got it. I also put in a call to the Bahamian authorities. Seems Pali got spooked when he saw the police coming at him at the marina. He… ate the partnership paperwork."

"What do you mean 'ate' it?" I grumbled, more than a little confused.

"I mean, he stuffed the thing into his mouth, chewed it to a pulp, and swallowed."

"Hm," Eugenia sniffed over my shoulder. "Surprised he managed to keep it down." I eyeballed her.

"So, unless this phantom drive shows up, my case is sinking faster than the Titanic," he said finally.

It wasn't dramatic. That was the problem.

Langley lowered his voice. "My supervisor called while I was out. Apparently, getting stabbed isn't a valid excuse for coming up empty."

Eugenia's jaw tightened. I felt something old and sour crawl up my spine.

"They're pulling me," Langley said. "If I go back without Bart's partner, without the drive, without the structure, this case gets reassigned. Or buried."

I leaned back against the wall, arms folded. "You didn't fail because you missed something. You failed because someone shishkabobbed you."

"Try putting that in a report."

He closed his eyes. When he opened them, he looked older than when we'd walked in.

"Thank you," he said. "Both of you. I know you didn't have to stay in this."

That hurt worse than blame.

My phone buzzed in my pocket.

I hadn't heard a peep out of the thing since we'd left Miami. At sea, you got spotty satellite service if you paid through the nose and stood in the right hallway, and even then it came and went like a bad conscience. I hadn't even gotten around to checking in with Gloria. I pulled it out anyway.

One email. Time-stamped hours ago.

Must've finally synced when we reboarded. Shore signal shaking hands with satellite lag. Technology had a cruel sense of timing.

Eugenia noticed my expression. Didn't ask.

"It's from Gloria," I said. "My daughter."

Langley looked away. He'd seen enough family fallout for one lifetime.

I opened it.

Dad. I don't know where you are or what you're doing, but you missed two calls and that never happens. Please tell me you're okay. I love you.

That was it.

No lecture. No accusation. Just fear dressed up as restraint.

I stared at the screen longer than necessary, then locked it and slid the phone back into my pocket.

"I should answer her," I said. "Before we lose signal again."

"Yes," Eugenia said softly. "You probably should."

We stepped out of med bay together. The corridor swallowed us whole—patterned carpet, fake art, soft lighting meant to soothe people who didn't want to think too hard about where they were.

Langley stayed behind. Powerless. Benched. Done.

I stopped walking.

Eugenia took two more steps before she realized and turned back.

"This is the part where we're supposed to have a breakthrough," I said. "The piece we missed. The thing that makes it all make sense."

She didn't argue. That hurt too.

Instead, she said, "Sometimes the board just clears itself."

"Not like this."

I thought of Gloria's message. Thought of Emma. Thought of all the times I'd sworn I was done with this sort of thing.

"I should've known better," I said. "Should've stayed retired."

Eugenia's eyes flashed. "You don't believe that."

"Today, I do."

We stood there longer than was comfortable, the ship

humming around us, pretending nothing important was happening in this very ugly hallway.

"I'm going to call my daughter," I said.

"Of course. Maybe we can meet up later? Discuss the case?"

"Yeah, I don't know. I'm feeling a little rundown." I hesitated. "Probably the sun. Think I might catch a few Zs."

"Sure," she murmured, but we both knew what I was really saying.

I waited for the itch. The old one. The urge to move, to press, to chase down one more angle before the trail went cold. It never showed. All I felt was the weight of everything we'd ruled out piling up where answers were supposed to be.

The board hadn't narrowed. It had wiped itself clean.

Somewhere behind us, a cart rattled. Ahead, laughter spilled out of an open lounge door, loud and unearned. *The Photuris* carried on, polished and indifferent, exactly as advertised.

I thought of Gloria's message again. Not the words — those were simple enough — but the space around them. The waiting. The fear she hadn't let herself write down.

"I don't think we missed a clue," I said finally. "I think we reached the end of what we're allowed to know."

Eugenia shifted her tote higher on her shoulder. "That's a grim thought."

"Retirement's full of them," I said. The line came out flatter than I meant it to.

I looked down the corridor, half expecting Langley to limp out after us, badge blazing, miracle in hand.

Instead, the door to med bay stayed closed. The ship chose motion over justice. Always had.

For the first time since this whole mess started, I understood something with uncomfortable clarity.

There was nothing left for me to do.

I stood there anyway.

That was when measured footsteps approached from behind — unhurried, deliberate, carrying the unmistakable weight of someone whose job description included endings.

I didn't turn around. I didn't need to.

Life had decided it was done letting us pretend we were in charge.

***

Captain Monty came at us hard, the way weather comes at a coastline. No warm-up. No pleasantries. Just a man in full uniform wearing the expression of someone who'd spent the last ten minutes explaining to his bridge crew that yes, this was ridiculous, and no, he did not enjoy being part of it.

He stopped in front of us and looked straight at me.

"Mrs. Drye."

Hy's posture tightened beside me. Monty flicked his eyes to him briefly, then back to me, as if Hy was an annoying footnote.

"I'm not your messaging service," he said. "I run a ship."

He said it the way some people said, "I run a prison."

I opened my mouth, but he kept going.

"And yet, somehow, I just got pulled into the middle of a domestic matter because your son decided the bridge was his personal reception desk."

My stomach dropped.

"My son—"

"Yes," Monty cut in. "Your son."

He reached into his jacket, produced a folded piece of paper, then hesitated as if the paper itself offended him.

"He called. Not guest services. Not the purser. The bridge." Monty's jaw worked once. "And before my officer could tell him we don't patch calls to passengers through the wheelhouse, Mr. Stewart Drye began reciting maritime policies, passenger safety language, and what I'm fairly sure were liability phrases designed to make my legal department wake up screaming."

Hy's mouth twitched. Not amusement. Recognition. He knew the type.

Monty continued, his voice rising by a fraction. "He referenced a 'welfare concern.' He used the words 'duty of care.' He implied repeatedly that if anything happened to you and it could be shown the ship ignored a credible report, certain parties would be 'very interested' in our handling of it."

He held the paper out to me between two fingers. Reluctant. Like a contaminated item.

"He made it clear," Monty said, "that he wasn't asking. He was documenting."

Heat climbed up my neck.

"How did he even know I was aboard? I didn't tell him where I was going," I said, because it mattered. It mattered to my pride if nothing else did.

Monty's expression did not soften. "If you plan to run away from home, you might not want to leave the brochure in the backseat."

"Oh," I said.

The word landed like a gavel.

Monty gave Hy a look that said this whole situation smelled like Hy's fault too, even if he couldn't quite prove it.

"And," Monty added, because of course there was more, "Mr. Drye says he will be waiting for you when we dock."

He paused, then — without any kindness at all — tacked on, "Both of you."

Hy's eyes narrowed. "He say that part too?"

Monty's mouth tightened. "He did. When I mentioned his mother was getting into all sorts of mischief with an older gentleman aboard ship, he was *very* interested in speaking with you, Mr. Reynolds. Firmly."

Then he shoved the message fully into my hand as if relieved to be rid of it.

"Read it. Don't read it. Frame it," he said. "But I suggest you handle your family business without involving my bridge again."

He turned on his heel and walked off, muttering under his breath about lawyers and nonsense and the ship apparently becoming a floating courthouse.

The corridor swallowed him.

And the folded paper in my hand suddenly weighed more than my tote ever had.

I stood there longer than necessary, staring at the carpet pattern like it might rearrange itself into better news. The looping navy-and-gold design blurred at the edges. I focused on it anyway, because focusing on anything else felt dangerous.

Hy stayed beside me. He didn't rush. He didn't fill the silence. He just waited, hands hooked into his pockets, shoulders squared in a way that meant he was bracing without knowing what for.

"He shouldn't know where I am," I said finally. "I didn't tell him."

Hy shifted his weight, the carpet giving a faint whisper under his shoes. "Then he worked it out," he said. No accusation. No curiosity. Just fact.

"Yes," I said. My throat tightened. "That sounds right."

I pictured Stewart without meaning to. Not angry. Never angry. Just disappointed in that precise, orderly way that made you want to line up your mistakes and label them correctly. I imagined him standing somewhere solid and immovable, waiting. He always waited. He believed that waiting proved a point.

"He thinks I've lost my judgment," I mumbled.

Hy didn't answer right away. He looked down the corridor instead, at nothing in particular. The patterned walls. The artificial lighting. The way the ship made everything feel temporary and sealed off from consequence.

This was usually the part where he said something. A theory. A correction. A half-joke that took the edge off.

Nothing came.

I let out a breath I hadn't realized I was holding. "He thinks I shouldn't be here."

Hy turned then, finally meeting my eyes. "Do you?"

The question landed harder than Stewart's message ever could have.

"I... I don't know," I said. And hated myself for how true that felt.

The silence that followed wasn't companionable. It was crowded. Full of second-guessing and old arguments and the growing suspicion that we had come all this way only to arrive at nothing.

The ship hummed around us. Lights glowed with artificial warmth. Somewhere nearby, a bell chimed for afternoon trivia.

The world continued with offensive cheer.

"That's it, then," I said.

He nodded once. Not looking at me. "Looks that way."

The words sat between us, unfinished.

"I didn't mean for this to happen," I said. "Any of it."

Hy exhaled slowly. "Nobody ever does."

Not sharp. Not kind. Just tired.

I swallowed. "I should've stayed in my lane."

That finally made him turn.

"Your lane? You shouldn't have even been on the freeway," he quipped, then paused. "For that matter, neither should I."

The words percolated for a moment or two before they just flat-out boiled over. I rolled my shoulders back and stood a little straighter.

"Now, hold on. We can do this. We were sticking to the map. Following the trail." I sniffed. "We just took a little detour is all." I brightened. "Like when you're on one of those family road trips, just trying to make it to the next rest stop, and you see that sign for world's largest ball of twine. You just have to stop, because when else are you going to get a chance to see the world's largest ball of twine. So, you take the exit."

"Yeah," Hy lifted his chin and looked me dead in the eye. "But you know what was at the end of this exit… a dead end."

The two words knocked the wind out of me. When I finally found my voice, it was small. "I thought we made a good team. I assumed we were helping."

"So did I." He chuckled, but there was absolutely no mirth in it. "I guess that makes me the ass."

He turned to leave. The furrow between my brows deepened. My chest heaved, hot air puffing from my nostrils.

"I'm starting to think maybe I'd be better off if I never met you, Hy Reynolds," I seethed at his back.

He stopped dead in his tracks and turned. "Yeah? Well, you've got no business trying to do real detective work, Jessica Fletcher."

I smiled. It was thin. Defensive.

"Is that so? Then, please… let me know when a real detective shows up, will you?"

"Fine."

"Fine."

We turned at the same time. He went left. I went right. The corridor swallowed us separately. The ship resumed its hum as though nothing of consequence had happened at all. And though I'd boarded the ship by myself, it was the first time I felt utterly, profoundly alone.

CHAPTER NINETEEN

I got to my stateroom like a man being chased, which was stupid considering the only thing after me was my own lousy mood. I slammed the door shut with more force than necessary and stood there a second, breathing through my nose, letting the ship's gentle sway try to talk me down.

It didn't work.

"Real smooth, Reynolds," I muttered to the empty room. "Top-notch exit."

The cabin smelled faintly of sunscreen, salt, and that lemon cleaner they used everywhere like it was a personality trait. I kicked off my sandals and immediately regretted it. Sand skittered across the floor in a dozen directions, sharp and gritty, announcing itself in places sand had no business being.

"Of course," I said. "Why wouldn't you follow me home?"

I stripped off my shorts and shook them once, twice — as if that might convince the sand to leave voluntarily. It responded by redistributing itself. The carpet. The bedspread. The chair. Everywhere. Tiny grains everywhere. Hundreds of them. Probably thousands. Enough to qualify as a small ecosystem.

I stared at the mess and snorted.

This was what I got for thinking I could play detective on vacation. This was what I got for not minding my own business. Gloria would have a field day with this. She'd say something calm and reasonable that somehow made me feel twelve years old and reckless all over again.

I bent to brush sand off my calf and missed a spot behind my knee. It scraped when I moved.

"Retirement," I said out loud. "They don't put *this* in the brochures."

I sat on the edge of the bed, elbows on my knees, and stared at the carpet like it might explain where the whole thing had gone sideways. Langley benched. Pali detained but not useful. Alicia loud and awful but clean where it mattered. Eugenia walking away down a corridor that suddenly felt longer than the ship itself.

I rubbed a hand over my face.

"What did you miss?" I asked the room.

The room, predictably, did not answer.

I stood back up and started pacing. Not fast. Just enough to keep my joints from filing a complaint. The ship hummed under my feet, steady and indifferent. I replayed Nassau like a bad movie I couldn't turn off.

Pali green as pond scum. The café. Alicia snapping orders like the world owed her a favor. The way she talked about money. Disposable. Not hers.

"The drive," I said. "Always about the drive."

227

I opened my drawer and dumped my pockets onto the desk. Keys. Wallet. A folded receipt. More sand. I brushed it aside with the side of my hand and frowned.

I toed off my socks and shook them once. Sand fell out like it had been waiting. I scowled at it, then froze.

Grains.

My mind snagged on the word and wouldn't let go.

Eugenia's voice floated up uninvited, calm and precise. Amarena syrup. Ground cherry pits. Almond scent. No sugar.

"No sugar," I repeated.

I straightened slowly.

If you were making syrup, real syrup, you'd have sugar. Plenty of it. Sticky. Granulated. Hard to hide. Harder to clean. It would cling to everything. Fingers. Glasses. Counters.

And yet...

I bent and rubbed the carpet between my fingers. Sand stuck. Sugar would have too.

Laila's bowl. Eugenia's description. Gritty. Pits. An almond scent.

I paced again, slower now, the irritation in my chest shifting shape.

"Who brought the drink?" I murmured.

The answer came quickly. Too quickly.

Laila.

I stopped pacing.

She had access. She had timing. And she had that quiet grief Eugenia mentioned. A Nonna. Lost savings. A heart that broke slowly instead of loudly.

Bart. His schemes. The way Langley said people lost

everything.

I exhaled.

Sand scratched under my heel.

I leaned my hands on the desk and stared at nothing, letting the pieces settle where they wanted instead of forcing them into place.

Laila didn't need cherries. She needed pits. She didn't need sugar. She needed bitterness. And she didn't need to touch the drink herself if she prepared the mix ahead of time.

Alicia couldn't be near cherries without puffing up. That wasn't drama. That was biology.

Which meant she hadn't made the deadly drink.

I let that sit for a minute.

Laila had.

I closed my eyes.

The blackout. The confusion. The way everyone assumed the loudest person in the room had done the worst thing. The way quieter people slipped past notice.

"That's on you," I told myself. "You should know better."

I straightened and rubbed at the back of my neck. The irritation was gone now, replaced by something sharper. Focused.

The sand on the floor didn't bother me anymore.

"Old dog," I growled. "Still got teeth."

I shoved my feet back into my sandals without bothering to clean them and reached for the door. I needed to find Eugenia. Only question was…*where in the hell was she?*

Alone with the failure.

I reached my cabin and shut the door softly. I leaned my back against it for a moment, eyes closed, listening to the low mechanical hum of the ship. It sounded steady. Confident. Like it knew where it was going even if the rest of us didn't.

"Well," I said to the room. "That went beautifully."

The cabin smelled faintly of citrus cleaner and sun-warmed fabric. The Caribbean sun sliced through the gauzy curtains across my balcony door.

I didn't feel sunshiny.

I set my tote down on the chair and toed off my shoes. My feet ached. Not sharply. Just enough to remind me I was not built for chasing criminals across tropical ports anymore.

I crossed to the vanity and stared at my reflection without quite meaning to. The lighting was unforgiving. Cruise ships had no interest in flattering anyone past forty.

Fine lines bracketed my mouth. The ones that deepened when I frowned. Which I did now, apparently out of habit.

"So," I spoke to the woman in the mirror. "What did we learn today?"

She looked tired. Pink blotches still ghosted her forearms beneath the calamine.

I turned one wrist, examining it critically.

We learned Pali was a thief with terrible balance. We learned Alicia was venomous but not lethal. We learned that Langley's case was slipping through our fingers like sand.

And we learned, most painfully of all, that enthusiasm did not count as evidence.

"I suppose this is the part where sensible people bow out," I muttered. "Go back to shuffleboard. Read by the pool. Stop pretending they are twenty years younger and sharper than they are."

The woman in the mirror did not nod.

I reached for the moisturizer, the one Hy had confiscated from Bart's room, because my skin felt tight and because I suddenly resented Alicia Bart for mentioning dry skin aging a woman faster than stress ever could.

As if any of us needed reminding.

The bottle's contents shifted strangely.

The sound registered somewhere low in my mind, beneath irritation and vanity and the dull ache of disappointment. I unscrewed the cap and tipped it slightly, waiting for the familiar resistance of thick cream.

Instead, something shifted inside.

A soft, unmistakable rattle.

I froze.

No. That was ridiculous.

I gave it a small shake.

Rattle.

I stared at the bottle. Then at my reflection again. The woman in the mirror looked at me like she was waiting for me to catch up.

The same sound as before.

"What is making that noise?" I asked slowly. I shook

the bottle again, harder this time.

Rattle. Thud.

Not liquid. Not air.

Something solid.

My pulse started galloping. I upended the bottle fully and squeezed the bottle over my palm. Lotion oozed out, pale and slick, pooling in my hand. Then it stopped.

I squeezed again.

Nothing.

"There should be more than that," I griped.

I frowned and peered into the opening. The inside was dark. Shadowed.

I turned the bottle upside down and tapped it against my palm.

Something slid free.

It landed with a wet, obscene plop.

I stared at it.

A small plastic bag. Sealed. Slippery with moisturizer. And inside it, unmistakable even through the haze of lotion, was a thumb drive.

The drive.

My breath left me in a rush.

"Oh," I said.

The word felt enormous.

For a moment, I simply stood there, lotion dripping between my fingers, staring at the thing that had been hiding in plain sight. All this time. First, with Hy. Then, in my bag. In my cabin. In my hand.

I set the bottle down carefully, as if sudden movement might undo the moment. I wiped my palm on a towel and picked up the bagged drive with reverent fingers.

It was small. Ordinary. The kind of thing you could lose between couch cushions or tuck into a pocket without thinking twice.

And yet it had been the fulcrum of everything. The missing piece Langley couldn't prove. The thing Alicia valued more than a million dollars. The reason Pali panicked. The reason Bart was dead.

I felt something loosen in my chest. Not relief. Something sharper.

Recognition.

"You didn't fail," I told myself quietly. "You just hadn't looked in the right place yet."

The realization did not make me feel clever. It made me feel angry.

Angry at Bart for hiding it this way. Angry at myself for dismissing the rattle. Angry at how close we had been to walking away.

I laughed once, short and incredulous.

"In moisturizer," I said. "Of course it was in moisturizer."

A place no one would search. A place no one would want to search.

A place people underestimated.

Just like the woman holding it.

I straightened and caught my reflection again. This time, the lines around my mouth looked different. Not softer. Firmer.

"You're not done," I said to her. "Not even close."

I slipped the drive into my pocket, lotion and all, and capped the bottle with shaking hands. My pulse thudded in my ears now, quick and insistent.

Hy.

He needed to know. Immediately.

I grabbed my tote and slung it over my shoulder, barely noticing the weight. The cabin suddenly felt too small. Too contained.

I had spent the last hour thinking we were finished.

We weren't finished. But if we didn't move fast, we would be too late.

I yanked the door open and stepped into the corridor without looking back.

The carpet swallowed my footsteps. The ship hummed around me, blissfully unaware that its carefully curated illusion had just cracked wide open.

"Don't you dare be sulking somewhere unreachable," I muttered, breaking into a brisk walk. "I do not have the patience for that tonight."

Passengers passed me, laughing, oblivious. Somewhere music thumped. Somewhere drinks clinked.

Somewhere on this ship, Hy Reynolds was questioning his instincts and his age and his place in the world.

I smiled grimly as I picked up speed.

"Hang on," I said aloud, earning a curious look from a passing couple. "The old girl isn't done yet."

For the first time since Nassau, the board had not cleared itself. It had been hiding its best move.

And I was going to make sure Hy was there to see it.

CHAPTER TWENTY

I rounded the corner like a man on a mission, which would've been impressive if sand wasn't still chafing my butt cheeks.

Instead, I walked straight into Eugenia Drye at full speed.

There was no graceful version of what happened next.

One second, I was muttering about sand in my privates and cherry pits. The next, the world tipped sideways and I was vaguely aware of elbows, tote straps, and a very unladylike sound that turned out to be me.

We went down in a heap.

Hard.

My shoulder hit carpet. Her knee hit something sensitive. A nearby decorative plant rattled in protest.

"Son of a—" I started.

"Do not finish that sentence," Eugenia snapped at the exact same time.

We lay there for half a beat, stunned, breathing hard, limbs tangled in a way that would've raised eyebrows if anyone had been around to see it.

Then her tote exploded. Not dramatically. Practically.

Contents skittered across the corridor: papers, sunglasses, a pen, a compact umbrella—and a lotion bottle that rolled away like it had someplace better to be.

Something clattered—plastic, sharp, distinct.

We both froze.

Slowly, Eugenia pushed herself upright, wincing. I did the same, rubbing my shoulder and glaring at the inanimate objects like they'd planned this.

"What were you doing?" I demanded.

She pointed at me. "What were *you* doing?"

"Walking."

"So was I."

"Well, clearly not well enough."

She reached for the tote at the same time I did.

Our hands collided again.

We both pulled back.

There between us on the carpet, slicked with lotion and shining under the corridor lights, sat a small plastic bag.

Inside it—we stared.

"No," I said.

"Oh, yes," Eugenia breathed, her blue eyes twinkling.

She picked it up carefully, like it might bite.

The thumb drive winked up at us, smug as hell.

"In the damned moisturizer," I muttered.

"I told you," she panted, still a little dazed. "That rattle wasn't normal."

I laughed. I couldn't help it. It burst out of me, sharp and disbelieving and just this side of hysterical.

Bart hadn't been sloppy.

He'd been clever.

I looked up at her. She was smiling too now. Small. Triumphant. Furious.

"Well," I said, hauling myself to my feet and offering her a hand, "I'll be a monkey's uncle."

She took it. Firm grip. Familiar.

"Nope," she declared and stood. "You are *definitely* not bananas, and neither am I."

We stood there a moment, catching our breath, the ship humming as if nothing important had just happened.

Then she squared her shoulders.

"We need to find Langley."

I nodded. "Immediately."

She tucked the drive into her pocket, wiped her hands on a napkin, and adjusted her tote like nothing in the world had gone wrong.

"Hy?"

"Yeah."

"Next time we run into each other," she rubbed her backside, "let's try not to do it horizontally."

"No promises," I said.

And this time, when we took off down the corridor together, we didn't split directions.

***

We were moving fast toward med bay, our footsteps falling into an uneven rhythm that matched the urgency humming under my skin. Hy leaned closer to me as we walked, voice pitched low.

"It was what you said earlier," he told me. "About the syrup."

I glanced at him. "The lack of sugar."

He nodded. "That. Syrup leaves traces. Sticky residue. Crystals. But you said there wasn't any. Just grit."

"The crushed cherry pit," I said.

"Exactly," he replied. "Ground too fine to be accidental."

I stopped short and slapped my palm lightly against my forehead. "Of course! Drupes!"

Hy frowned. "I'm sorry?"

"Drupes!" I pressed on, words tumbling out now that the shape of it had finally snapped into focus. "Thin outer skins, fleshy middle. Single hard pit in the center."

"You calling me a drupe?"

"No, no, no," I said, waving that aside. "A drupe is a fruit! Like cherries. Crushing the pits yields amygdalin. It's a cyanogenic glycoside. Enzymatic breakdown releases hydrogen cyanide. I read a delightful botany book on it at the library."

Hy let out a quiet huff. "Yeah, well, that's all fine and dandy, but I was just thinking about a case I worked where a guy accidentally poisoned his neighbor's dog because he didn't seal his trash can lid. Dog got into a bunch of cherry pits. Vet was able to pump the dog's stomach, thank God, but it got me thinking."

We started walking again, faster now.

"I don't think Laila was making her Nonna's syrup at all," Hy said. "I think she was crushing the pits to get that, what did you call it — Cyrano de Bergerac —"

"Cyanogenic glycoside."

"Yeah," he said. "That stuff—she put it in Bart's drink."

The corridor seemed to narrow around us.

Laila. Quiet. Efficient. Always nearby without ever being in the way. The kind of person people trusted because she made herself small.

"We need to tell Langley," I said.

"Now," Hy agreed.

That was when laughter slammed into us from the side.

High-pitched. Unrestrained. Fueled by alcohol and poor judgment.

The bachelorette party.

Pink sashes. Plastic tiaras. Someone shrieking about lost shoes. Another woman spun sideways, nearly colliding with Hy.

"Oh my God, sorry!" one of them cried, grabbing my arm like we were suddenly co-conspirators.

"Hey!" One inebriated ponytail leaned in and squinted at Hy. "Weren't you one of our strippers last night?"

Hy couldn't suppress the mischievous grin that spread across his face.

"Ladies." Hy tipped his hat and stepped back, guiding me with him as we veered into the nearest open corridor to avoid being trampled by a woman wielding a novelty cup shaped like a pineapple.

The laughter echoed behind us as we escaped. I checked over my shoulder. We were losing time.

The hallway we stumbled into looked identical to the

last one. Same carpet. Same lighting. Same soft, deceptive calm. We walked briskly for several seconds before Hy slowed.

"This isn't right," he said.

I looked around. No med bay signage. No helpful arrows. Just doors. Endless doors.

"We turned," I said. "Didn't we?"

"I thought we did."

The realization settled between us.

The ship had done what this case had been doing to us for the better part of the cruise.

It had rearranged us.

The carpet ended abruptly, replaced by smooth tile that reflected overhead lights far too well. The air sharpened — cleaner, hotter — laced with the ghost of fresh herbs and oil. The culinary demonstration kitchen.

The glass-fronted room opened ahead, all stainless steel and precision. Counters gleamed. Everything ready. Nothing in motion.

Knives hung magnetized along the wall. "Oh," I said. "This looks dangerous."

"Perfect," Hy muttered. "We solve the case and get lost doing it."

I opened my mouth to reply — and slammed right into an unyielding body.

CHAPTER TWENTY-ONE

"Laila."

I said her name the moment we stepped into the demo kitchen. Not loud. Not sharp. Just enough to set it down between us and see what it did to the air.

While she looked up, I clocked everything else without meaning to. Stainless steel everywhere. Counters too solid to soften a fall. A floor that would hurt if you hit it wrong. And knives — too many of them — laid out neat and proud like they were part of the décor instead of a bad idea waiting for timing.

My body did the math before my head caught up. Two exits. One closer than the other. Distance to the door. Distance to the counter. Distance to her. I shifted half a step forward, grumbling under my breath about getting turned around again, like this was just another inconvenience on a ship full of them.

It wasn't.

I put myself slightly in front of Eugenia without making a thing of it. Old habit. Same one that told me where not to stand and who not to turn my back on. I angled my shoulder just enough to block the knife strip from her line of sight, like I was shielding her from nothing more than a bad layout choice.

Bad room, I thought.

Very bad room.

Laila started talking. Same tone she always used. Calm. Polite. Familiar enough to make people lower their guard without realizing they'd done it.

I didn't listen to a word of it.

I watched her hands.

They moved easily around the prep station, as if they belonged there. Fingers hovering near a knife without hesitation. No flinch. No pullback. Just comfort. Ownership. The kind that comes from repetition, not nerves.

That told me more than her voice ever could.

This wasn't fear. And it sure as hell wasn't surprise.

"You didn't just happen to run into us, did you?" I asked.

She didn't bother pretending. Just let out a small breath and tipped her head a fraction, like I'd finally asked the polite question instead of the real one.

"No," she said. "I didn't stumble into you."

Her hands folded together, then unfolded again. Still loose. Still steady.

"I've been keeping a close eye on you since the stabbing," she went on. "Trying to ferret out how much you knew. I overheard you when you got back from the shore excursion. Thought maybe I was in the clear."

I felt Eugenia shift beside me. Didn't look. Didn't

move.

Laila smiled then, just a little. "I was even on my way to bring you a bottle of my Nonna's Amarena Syrup, Mrs. Drye." She gestured to the bottle sitting innocuously on a nearby stainless steel counter.

I made a face before I could stop myself.

"But I saw you fly out of your cabin like it was on fire," she continued, unbothered. "Figured I'd better follow you. See what's what."

Her gaze flicked to Eugenia. Softened.

"You remind me a lot of her, you know."

Her hands never stopped moving.

Eugenia took the lead without asking. She always did when she wanted answers instead of reactions. I stayed where I was, half a step forward, close enough to matter. Close enough to end it if I had to.

"Laila," Eugenia said, voice calm, almost kind. "Walk me through it."

Laila didn't flinch. She didn't bristle. She smiled faintly, the way someone does when they think they're being understood.

"Which part?" she asked.

"Bart," Eugenia said. "First."

Laila exhaled slowly. Not guilty. Resolute.

"That wasn't messy," she said. "It was quiet. Clean. He drank. He complained about the heat. Then he didn't get back up."

I watched her hands as she spoke. They stayed relaxed. No tremor. No reach toward the knives. That told me more than her words ever could.

"And Langley?" Eugenia asked.

That smile slipped. Just a fraction.

"That wasn't supposed to happen," Laila said. "Not like that."

"You stabbed him," I stated — not accusing. Just placing the fact on the counter between us.

Her eyes flicked to me. Then back to Eugenia.

"Yes," she said. "Because he wouldn't stop asking questions. Because he kept circling Bart's finances. Because if he followed that trail far enough — " She shrugged, small. Controlled. "He would have found me."

"So, you escalated," I said.

"I protected myself," she replied. "The murder was finished. The stabbing was prevention — insurance."

Eugenia nodded once, like she was aligning puzzle pieces in her head.

"You weren't angry," she said. "You were afraid."

Laila met her gaze. "Fear is much more useful."

I felt my jaw tighten. This wasn't a woman unraveling. This was a woman who'd planned every step and only stumbled once.

And now she knew we'd caught up.

I shifted my weight, subtle, putting more of myself between her and the room.

Because this part of the conversation?

This was where things usually went bad.

***

I saw it before it happened.

Not the decision — that had already been made — but the shift. The moment her body stopped listening to conversation and started listening to instinct. Laila's shoulders lowered. Her weight rolled forward onto the balls of her feet. Her hands, which had been so careful, so contained, suddenly chose a direction.

Toward me.

I did not freeze. That surprised me later.

In the moment, there was no panic. Just clarity. Years of watching people—really watching them—had taught me that violence rarely announces itself with shouting. It arrives quietly, already in motion.

I stepped sideways instead of back.

My heel clipped the wheel of the rolling prep cart beside me. I shoved it hard. Not graceful. Not strong. Just decisive. The cart skidded across the tile with a metallic shriek, slamming into Laila's shin and breaking her stride.

She swore. Momentum betrayed her.

That half a second mattered.

Behind me, Hy moved at the same instant. I felt him there, solid and fast, exactly where I needed him to be without ever having to ask. But I didn't stop moving. I knew better than that.

"Laila," I said, keeping my voice level as my heart pounded. "Don't."

She recovered quickly—too quickly for someone untrained—but frustration cracked through her composure now. Her hand closed around the handle of a pan sitting on the counter. Heavy. Cast iron.

Not decorative.

I angled away, keeping the prep table between us. Distance mattered. Distance was survival. I had no intention of testing my reflexes against her reach.

"You don't want this," I said, circling slowly, eyes never leaving her hands.

"You're right," she panted. "I don't. I didn't want Nonna to die either, but that man, Bart, he had taken everything from her. It wasn't fair he got to live, and she didn't."

My heart went out to her. The pain was etched on my face. "But revenge? This doesn't end the way you think it does."

Her breathing was sharp now. Uneven.

"You don't understand," she snapped.

"I understand perfectly," I said. "I understand how alone you feel." I looked at Hy. "More than you know."

That landed. I saw it.

She lunged again—but this time Hy was ready. The pan swung wide, glancing off the stainless-steel counter instead of flesh. The sound rang through the room, loud and final.

I stayed on my feet. I stayed out of reach. And even as the situation turned physical, even as my pulse roared in my ears, I understood something with startling calm.

This wasn't about strength. It never was.

It was about who kept thinking, when everything else went wrong.

The pan came up fast.

Too fast.

There was no room left to sidestep, no cart to shove, no clever angle to exploit. Just cast iron arcing toward my head with the kind of grim certainty that ends conversations permanently.

I remember thinking, with astonishing clarity, *Well. This is inconvenient.*

Then something dark and glassy entered my field of vision from the side.

There was a dull, wet crack—less cinematic than you'd hope—and Laila made a small, surprised sound, almost polite, before her knees gave out beneath her. The pan clattered to the floor, spinning once before settling.

She collapsed in a heap at my feet.

I stood there, frozen, breath locked in my chest, staring down at her slack form.

Hy stood beside me, holding the shattered remains of a bottle of Amarena syrup by the neck. Red liquid dripped steadily onto the tile, pooling around the shards of glass like something symbolic I didn't have time to unpack.

"Pour some sugar on me," he said, voice gruff and perfectly unimpressed.

I stared at him.

"You hit her," I said faintly.

"Correct," he replied. "With drupe fruit."

Before I could respond, the door to the demo kitchen burst open.

Captain Monty stormed in at full sail, hat askew, face already flushed with fury. The chef followed close behind, white coat flapping, eyes widening at the sight of the unconscious woman on the floor, the blood-colored syrup, the broken bottle, and Hy Reynolds standing there looking like he was ready to rumble with the Jets.

"What—" Monty began, then stopped, hands flying up. "What in God's name is happening *on my ship*?"

Hy glanced down at the bottle, then back at Monty. "Long story," he said. "Short version — she tried to brain us."

The chef made a strangled noise.

Monty rubbed his face with both hands, then pointed at us without looking. "Nobody moves," he barked. "Nobody speaks. And if either of you breathes a word about this, I swear I will personally throw you overboard."

I exhaled for the first time in what felt like hours.

Laila didn't move.

And for the first time since this nightmare began, neither did the case.

EPILOGUE

The Photuris slid toward Miami like nothing bad had ever happened on her decks.

No blood. No screaming. No poison. Just sunshine, steel drums piping in through the open promenade doors, and a ship full of passengers who looked refreshed instead of traumatized. If you didn't know better, you'd think this entire trip had been exactly what the brochure promised.

I *did* know better.

Eugenia stood beside me at the rail, hands folded tight around her tote strap. She was smiling, but it had a brittle edge to it, the way people smile when they're pretending their pulse isn't doing something athletic.

"Bit jumpy there," I said.

"I am not jumpy," she replied. "I am… aware."

That might have had something to do with the two very large security officers flanking us like decorative bookends.

Captain Monty loomed a few feet back, arms crossed, expression locked into what I'd come to recognize as *I am done with this nonsense.*

"I am going to make absolutely certain you two get off this ship," he'd informed us earlier.

Then, for emphasis:

"Thank God I'm getting a new assignment. Hopefully, there won't be meddling busybodies on that ship."

I took that as a compliment.

It wasn't all bad news. Langley had gotten the drive. His supervisors were suddenly very interested in his survival instincts and much less interested in his earlier mistakes. From what he told us, most of Bart's victims were likely to see some form of restitution.

Justice, the slow kind. The kind that counts.

Langley had shaken my hand, then Eugenia's, his grip firmer than it had been in days.

"Thanks," he said. "Both of you. And hey — maybe we'll run into each other again someday."

I raised an eyebrow.

"Preferably without murder or attempted murder."

He winced. "Yes. Let's aim for that."

Now the horn sounded. The dock crept closer. Miami waited.

Real life.

I glanced sideways at Eugenia. "You ready for it?"

She followed my gaze toward the shore.

Gloria stood there, patient as ever, arms folded, scanning the crowd with that particular look that said she already knew exactly how much trouble I'd been in.

Eugenia inhaled. "Bingo nights and quilting circles?" she said. "Bite your tongue."

"Yeah," I muttered. "Me neither."

The gangway lowered with a mechanical whine.

Time to disembark.

Time to behave.

But then, Gloria caught my eye. She had started walking toward me, her expression looking an awful lot like mine used to when I'd walk into an interrogation room, when she stopped. She noticed Eugenia, and her head tilted a fraction of an inch.

She held my gaze. All I could do was shrug.

A small smile played about the edges of her lips. She raised a hand and just… waved.

I waved back.

I chuckled, more at the fact that I had been worried for even a second that my daughter wouldn't understand me.

Eugenia, however, wasn't getting off that easy.

***

I spotted Stewart before he spotted me.

Which meant I had approximately three seconds.

The taxi screeched up to the curb like it was late for something important. The door flew open and Stewart launched himself out, scanning the crowd with surgical precision.

Then he saw me.

"Mother!" he called, already moving. I ducked my head, pulling the brim of my sunhat down. When I dared peek, Stewart was scowling.

Hy turned. "That your boy?"

"Yes," I sighed.

Stewart was already was already waving.

"Keep moving," I whispered to Hy.

He didn't ask questions. He never did when it mattered. And that was just one of the things I was really starting to like about him.

We veered sideways, broke formation, and lunged toward a different waiting taxi just as Stewart's voice rose behind us in outraged disbelief.

"Eugenia Murgatroyd Drye!"

Hy looked at me in quizzical disbelief. "Your middle name is Murgatroyd?"

"Zip it, or you're going to be the next body," I warned and shoved him in the waiting taxi.

The door slammed. The car lurched forward.

The driver glanced at us in the mirror. "Where to?"

I didn't hesitate. "The nearest travel agent."

Hy let out a bark of laughter.

The driver squinted. "Y'all aren't thinkin' of takin' another cruise, are you? Heard there was a murder and a stabbing on this one. And my cousin just told me about another ship — *The Lampyris*. Bunch of weird accidents. I'm tellin' yea, cruise ships are dangerous places, man."

I caught Hy's eye.

He grinned.

"Don't we know it," I said, giving him a wink — picturing the exact ship we'd be sailing away on next.

The taxi sped off.

Behind us, Miami receded.

Ahead of us?

Well…

Let's just say retirement had officially left the harbor.

About the Author

Maisie Franklin believes life's best mysteries are solved with wit, wine, and just the right splash of snark. A firm believer that trouble pairs best with a full-bodied red, she writes character-driven cozy mysteries packed with sharp banter, clever puzzles, and sleuths who are just as likely to argue their way to the truth as stumble into it.

When she's not plotting the downfall of an unsuspecting culprit, Maisie can be found outsmarting crossword puzzles, getting far too emotionally invested in British baking competitions, or insisting that "just one more chapter" is a perfectly reasonable life choice. She's a lifelong mystery lover, an unapologetic pun enthusiast, and the kind of friend who would absolutely help you plan the perfect alibi — strictly hypothetically, of course.

Whether she's exploring shipside secrets, small-town scandals, or crimes that refuse to stay politely solved, Maisie's stories always come with a side of humor, heart, and the occasional exasperated investigator along for the ride. Pour yourself a glass, settle in, and enjoy — there's always another mystery waiting.

Cozy Crimes, Clever Clues, and a Dash of Attitude

Want to stay afloat with what's coming next from Maisie? Subscribe to *The Wine & Crimes Club* Newsletter for freebies, updates, and sometimes just a decent wine recommendation.

Scan me

-OR-

https://maisiefranklinauthor.wordpress.com/

Other Books by Maisie Franklin

THE AUGUR'S ASSASSIN: A READ BETWEEN THE VINES MYSTERY

Murder wasn't in the cards... until it was.

Zoe Romano gave up front-page crime for fine wine, trading the chaos of New York City for the quiet charm of Mystic, Connecticut. Now, she runs Read Between the Vines, a cozy bookshop-slash-wine bar where the biggest scandal is usually who finished the last bottle of merlot.

That is, until the town psychic turns up dead — with a tarot card stuck in her throat.

Everyone in Mystic had a reason to want Madame Zorina to zip it, but only one of them is a killer. And when Chief of Police Derek Cody enlists Zoe's help, she and her meddling staff start uncorking Mystic's best-kept secrets. And a few missing lawn flamingos.

Between pouring wine, dodging well-intentioned chaos,

and making sure her own fate doesn't end up in the death card pile, Zoe will need every ounce of wit—and maybe a splash of luck—to solve this case. Because in Mystic, murder might be in the cards… but Zoe refuses to let fate call the shots.

AVAILABLE NOW!

Scan me

Coming Soon!

HYDRANGEAS, HYACINTHS & HOMICIDE: A HETTY HUDSON HORTICULTURAL MYSTERY

She may have a green thumb… but he's got a nose for murder.

In the quaint village of Alder Grove, florist Hetty Hudson is known for her eye for beauty and her talent for floral design — especially when it comes to weddings.

But when a local historian turns up dead in the church garden just days before a lavish wedding, Hetty's peaceful arrangements are uprooted by a growing tangle of secrets. Armed with nothing but a keen intuition, a sharp wit, and her encyclopedic knowledge of flower symbolism, Hetty and her precocious tabby, Winston, dig into old grudges, buried family feuds, and a mystery that smells more like cover-up than compost. With wedding bells clashing against murder investigations, Hetty must act fast to ensure the only bouquet being tossed isn't resting on a casket.

Hydrangeas, Hyacinths, and Homicide is a warm, witty, and whimsically dangerous cozy mystery — a blooming start to a horticultural sleuth series that promises bouquets, backstabbing, and bloomers caught in the bushes.

www.ingramcontent.com/pod-product-compliance
Lightning Source LLC
Chambersburg PA
CBHW020317200626
46814CB00006BA/2285